Also from Dagger Books
by Christine Husom

Murder In Winnebago County

Buried in Wolf Lake

By

Christine Husom

Dagger Books
Published by Second Wind Publishing, LLC.
Kernersville

Dagger Books
Second Wind Publishing, LLC
931-B South Main Street, Box 145
Kernersville, NC 27284

First Dagger Books edition published August, 2009.
Dagger Books, Running Angel, and all production design are trademarks of Second Wind Publishing, used under license.

For information regarding bulk purchases of this book, digital purchase and special discounts, please contact the publisher at www.secondwindpublishing.com

Manufactured in the United States of America

ISBN 978-1-935171-35-5

To my beautiful, multi-talented, hard-working mother who knew what was important and taught by example.

ACKNOWLEDGMENTS
To Niki Turner for superb editing, to Richard Haskin
for another beautiful cover, to Mike Simpson, Tracy
Beltran, and the Second Wind authors for continued
help, to my family and friends for their unselfish love
and unending support.
Thanks, Chris

PROLOGUE

From a distance he wouldn't have been able to tell them apart, even if they were standing side by side. Eve's twin. He could easily take her for the evening and keep her for all eternity. He continued to stare as he got closer. He wasn't imagining things. Definitely Eve.

Damn! He waited too long and didn't move in fast enough. Someone else got her attention and whisked her away. Where to, he didn't know. He couldn't think about that. There was no reason to get upset. He knew who she was and he'd be back for her. If not later that night, then the next one, or the one after that.

Impatience could never get in the way of his mission. Following the steps in the plan, one by one, was key to success.

There were plenty of fish in the Hennepin Avenue sea. He went back to searching. It was possible there was another one out there. He looked for another hour, but none of them fit Eve's description.

He'd find her, it just might take a little time. Meanwhile, he had videos to take the edge off his hunger.

1.

"Sergeant Aleckson, report to my office." Sheriff Twardy's voice dropped like a bomb from the public address system speaker in the squad room where four other Winnebago County deputies and I worked on reports.

Instead of phoning or paging me, the sheriff always called me over the rarely used system, letting everyone in the department know I was sumoned *again*. He didn't do it to humiliate me. The sheriff was in his late fifties and old-school cop in many ways.

As I hit "save" on the computer and pulled out the zip drive, the chiding began.

"Wha'd you do this time, Corinne?" Brian Carlson mocked, throwing his head to the side to look at me.

I wracked my brain for a second and shrugged. "I honestly don't know." *For once.* "You guys can stop your gloating. I'll tell you when I get back." I stacked my reports and shoved them to the side.

"You mean *if* you get back," Todd Mason paused from his typing to dig in.

"Very funny, Mason. You know, I really love the moral support you give me around here. Remember, what goes around comes around. Next time once of you guys gets called before the sheriff—"

"Are you kidding? Hey, we're not the ones who are always getting ourselves in trouble—you are," Todd shot back.

I looked back over my shoulder as I crossed the threshold. "Only because, as your sergeant, I take the heat and keep you out of it."

"Whatever," Todd murmured.

"Huh!" Brian added.

As I wove my way to the sheriff's office, I reflected on the camaraderie I had with most of the other deputies in the department. A few weeks before, Mason and Carlson helped stop a madwoman intent on killing my friend and me. I hoped I would never have to return the favor, but we all knew I wouldn't hesitate if it came to that.

"Denny, there is no way she is going in there!"

I heard Detective Elton Dawes' voice resound from the sheriff's office.

"That's not up to you, Smoke! It's up to her. You're too protective of Aleckson. She *is* a trained professional, for godsakes," Sheriff Twardy shot back.

Oh, boy, now what? Everyone in the secretarial pool was, no doubt, as curious as I was about the exchange. I knocked, stepped inside, and closed the door before more words could escape into the outer office. The sheriff's hazel eyes and Smoke's sky blues fixed on me.

Instead of demanding to know what was going on, I politely said, "Yes, sir?"

"Take a seat, Sergeant."

I eased onto a chair across from the sheriff. The creases in his face seemed deeper than usual. Twardy continued to scrutinize me and I fought the urge to shift in my seat. I glanced at Smoke. He was looking down and running his hands through his thick salt and pepper hair. *What was going on?*

"I got a call from Captain Palmer," the sheriff said.

Palmer was the administrator of the Winnebago County Jail.

"Alvie Eisner wants to see you. Alone." Sheriff Twardy watched for my reaction.

I tried to mentally process why Alvie Eisner would possibly want to see me. *Alone.*

Smoke leaned forward. "Forget it! That monster almost killed Corky and now she wants to see her? Just forget it." He looked from me to the sheriff. His long dimples deepened as he worked the muscles in his lean, angular face.

I tuned out Twardy's and Smoke's voices as visions of Alvie Eisner jumped to life in my mind. Her only son, a miscreant, had been sent to prison for his crimes and committed suicide while incarcerated. Alvie determined revenge would be best served by killing everyone she held responsible for his death. She murdered a retired judge, the county attorney, and the public defender. It was sweeter still when she made the deaths look like suicides so their families would suffer as she had.

Due to my level of involvement in the investigation, Alvie Eisner determined I should die too. She threatened my friend Sara, a probation officer, and me with a gun. When I knocked the gun out of her hands, she went after me with the full force of her body. Eisner was many inches taller and close to one hundred pounds heavier, so she was a worthy adversary. I battled Alvie Eisner for a matter of minutes, but they were very, very long minutes. Thank God my colleagues arrived when they did.

A little more than a month later, I continued to wake from terrifying nightmares in a cold sweat, with my heart pounding. I knew I should talk to someone about my dreams, but I wasn't ready. The thought of putting words to my angst sent waves of increased anxiety through my entire body. I shuddered slightly.

"That woman is out of her gourd." I came back to Smoke's words. "There is no reason she should be allowed to talk to Corky. She'll face her in court when Corky testifies against her. They can't discuss the case, so what in the hell could she possibly want?"

"Palmer told me Eisner said it was something personal—not about the case."

Smoke craned his neck toward the sheriff. "Personal? *Personal*? She is totally off her rocker if she thinks Corky wants to discuss anything *personal* with her."

The sheriff and Smoke were both right. Alvie was off her rocker and Smoke—my mentor and dear friend— had always been a little protective of me. He was even more so after the incident with Eisner.

"I'm here," I reminded the men, interrupting their

stalemate. "Okay, I agree. Alvie Eisner is a monster, but I can't help but wonder what she wants. I mean, don't you?" I looked from Smoke to the sheriff, but neither replied.

I continued, "I don't think I heard five sentences come out of her mouth through our entire investigation. I was lucky to get a 'yes' or 'no' the times I talked to her."

"Bad, bad idea," Smoke said.

"I'll tell Palmer I'll meet with Eisner after her trial is over with. The jail can shackle her. We'll be on opposite sides of a heavy conference table. Someone can watch through the glass."

Smoke crossed his hands on his chest. "I still say no. She's a damn nut case."

"That's a news flash!" I waved my hands in front of me like I was holding a newspaper. "We'll have the jail strip search her before the interview, check for hidden weapons—"

My words were interrupted by the sheriff's phone.

"Sheriff Twardy . . . What! . . . Tell me again . . . What's the location? . . .Okay." I watched the sheriff's face grow red, the visible sign his blood pressure was climbing. He stood and straightened to his full five-foot-eight-inch height.

"Call the mobile crime lab. Who's working major crimes this week, again?. . . Okay, good. I got Dawes and Aleckson with me. They'll meet the crime lab team out there. Send the call information to the squad computers, but don't put this out on the radio. Flag it as confidential. We'll find out what we got first." The sheriff hung up and shook his head. Silver-gray hair framed his red face.

Smoke's body tensed during the sheriff's conversation and my own muscles tightened in turn.

"That was communications. This is a new one. A dog just came home with a human leg, appears to be from a female."

"Where?" Smoke asked.

"Dayton Township, Wolf Lake. You two get a move on. I'll see you there." The sheriff led the way out of his office and stopped by his secretary's desk to fill her in.

"I gotta grab my reports from the squad room. Beat you there," I challenged Smoke.

"Yeah, right."

Smoke was, hands down, the most skilled driver in the department. He could push one hundred miles an hour on curvy roads. All the deputies were good, but no one was that good.

The squad room was empty so I grabbed my things without needing to converse. I hustled to my squad car. "608, Winnebago County."

"Go ahead, 608," communications officer Robin answered.

"I'm clear 10-19."

"10-4, at 1530."

Winnebago County had recently equipped our squad cars with portable computers linked to the county communications department, sheriff's report and arrest records, as well as Minnesota state driver and vehicle registration records. I read the call for service on my computer.

The reporting person was a Tara Engen of 8539 Abbott Avenue Northwest, Dayton Township. Not a name I recognized. There were a number of people who called in to report various extraordinary, sometimes downright unbelievable, things on a regular basis. They were seldom valid complaints. Some of the callers had mental health issues. Others were bored, hyper-vigilant, or just plain too nosy for their own good. But, like the little boy who cried wolf, even our frequent theatrical reporters had a legitimate call from time to time.

It was a suspicious circumstances call. Tara Engen reported her dog found a woman's leg in Wolf Lake. My mind scanned through reports of missing people in the county. We had our fair share. Most were teenagers who left without telling their parents where they were going and turned up a day or two later. There was the occasional dementia patient who wandered off on foot or in the family car. The majority were found fairly quickly.

Once in a while, a non-custodial parent would run off with his or her child. But a missing woman? I could not recall one in the recent past.

How long had the leg been in the water? Days, months, years?

Suspicious circumstances, all right.

A message from Smoke appeared on my screen. "20?" He wondered where I was.

"CR 10, at 50th." I typed back with my right hand, keeping the squad car under control with my left.

"10-4, crossing 70th."

Smoke was two miles ahead of me. I pushed down my accelerator, knowing I wouldn't catch up with him, but I could try. Wolf Lake was about twelve miles from the station. Officially, it wasn't a red lights and siren call, but to the person keeping watch over a woman's leg, it would be. The faster we got there, the better.

"710, Winnebago County." It was Deputy Todd Mason on the radio.

"Go ahead, 710," Robin answered for communications.

"Show 710 and 723 10-8 with Unit 3." Mason and Carlson were rolling with the mobile crime lab.

"10-4, at 1539."

Dayton Township was sparsely populated. Lake Pearl State Park occupied about half the nine square mile area. Lowlands, unsuitable for building or farming, took up another quarter. The remaining ground was rolling tree-covered hills, pastures, and farm fields. The south and west sides of Wolf Lake butted up to the state park.

County Road 10 crossed County Road 27 on the southern border of the Minnesota state park. I slowed down as I approached County Road 27 and turned left. Abbott Avenue was the first cross road and I pulled my steering wheel right. It was a gravel road and dust hung in the air from a vehicle ahead of me. My squad car stirred up more. I saw nothing but a cloud behind me when I glanced in the rear view mirror. I crossed Eighty-fifth Street Northwest, the road that led into the park.

Abbott ran close to the west bank of Wolf Lake and I surveyed the water as I drove by, half expecting a hand to pop up like in the old movie, *Deliverance*. What had happened to the rest of the woman? Coyotes? Cougars? Coyotes were prevalent and the Minnesota Department of Natural Resources reported occasional cougar sightings. Either was possible, but would an animal leave a leg in the lake? Not likely.

I continued to the north side of the lake and pulled into the Engen's driveway. An older yellow farmhouse sat on a small rise with a barn and several outbuildings. It was the only dwelling on the lake, built many years before the state purchased the nearby land for the park in the 1960s.

I phoned communications to tell them I had arrived and hopped out of my car. A dog barked in the distance, perhaps from the barn, or a kennel behind the house. He sounded big enough to carry a woman's leg in his mouth.

Smoke and a forty-something brunette woman stood together near some patio furniture on the east side of the house. Actually, Smoke stood and the woman rolled from feet flat on the ground to tippy-toes in a continual rocking motion. Her arms crossed her body in a self hug as she peered at the ground.

Smoke looked at me as I approached, creased his eyebrows together then blinked at a spot a few feet away. I fixed my eyes on the gruesome sight of a woman's right leg–from the tips of her scarlet red polished toenails to the top of the thigh. The cut which severed the leg from the rest of the body was clean, not jagged or ragged or torn. Not the work of an animal–a non-human animal, at least.

"Mrs. Engen–Tara–why don't you have a seat on the chair, there," Smoke directed in a calming tone. He put a hand on Engen's shoulder to guide her to the patio furniture.

Engen released a loud breath. She stopped rocking, but shook her hands at her sides for some seconds. "Um . . . I'm gonna be sick."

She ran a short distance and retched a few times before vomiting. I swallowed and slowly sucked in air through my nose to calm my own churning stomach. Smoke's eyes traveled from Engen, to the ground and back, for the duration of her sick spell.

Engen's peaked face was splotched with red circles when she finished. "Okay if I go get cleaned up?"

"Of course," Smoke assured her.

Smoke and I moved closer to the leg. "Hopefully, she'll be feeling a little better now," Smoke said.

"Don't count on it. Not for a long, long time," I countered.

The grass on the lawn was recently cut, a neatly trimmed combination of grass, clover, and plantain. The pale white leg with its red toenails, on a bed of green grass, struck a frightful contrast. The colors of Christmas on a warm August day.

"Okay, this is the creepiest thing I have ever seen," I said.

"I got a lot more years in than you so I'd have to think about that." Smoke squatted to get a closer look and moved the readers from his breast pocket to his face. "Yeah, I'd say this would be on my top ten list. Let's see what we got here."

I could observe perfectly well from where I stood.

"Pretty clean cut. Power saw? Miter saw, fine blade? A butcher's saw?" he guessed. "Appears to be from a fairly young Caucasian woman--I don't know, twenties, thirties. Takes care of herself: pedicure, shaved, maybe waxed, legs--or leg--to be precise."

Smoke squinted against the sun to find my face. "Which brings up the obvious question. Where the hell is the rest of her?"

I glanced around, taking in the surroundings. The yard was mowed to a few feet from the water. Swamp grasses filled the space between the lawn and the lake. Poplars grew close to the water on the east bank. Pines and hardwoods--maple, oak, and basswood of the state park–filled in behind them.

Where *was* the rest of the victim's body and how did her leg wind up in a small, rural Winnebago County lake?

"Wha'd Engen say?" I asked.

"Not much. I got here only a minute before you. Said her Golden went for a swim and came back with the leg." Smoke studied the leg for a few seconds. "Doesn't look like it's been in the water long. I'd say we got ourselves a crime scene."

"You can see the dog's teeth marks, but look–" I had grown more accustomed to the sight and squatted, facing Smoke on the other side of the leg, "–it looks like a human bite mark here."

I pointed to the spot near the top of the thigh. The injured area was several inches in diameter. There were bruise marks where it appeared six upper and six lower teeth had sunk into the victim's flesh.

Smoke lowered his head for a better look. "Yeah, well somebody likes to play way, way too rough–bites and cuts."

I heard a vehicle on the gravel. The dog, which had quit barking some minutes before, started up again.

"Crime lab is here," I said.

We stood and Smoke waved the deputies over. "Grab the tape and some stakes," he called.

Brian Carlson opened the side door of the mobile unit, stepped in and out a second later with a roll of bright yellow crime scene tape and a small armful of thin, metal stakes.

Mason walked up to the dismembered leg and shook his head. "This is the stuff nightmares are made of."

Smoke nodded. "No doubt."

"Mine are bad enough already," I said.

Smoke opened his mouth in question as Sheriff Twardy's unmarked white Crown Victoria pulled in and parked next to my squad car in the driveway. He climbed out and hurried over.

"Had to get gas," he said in case anyone wondered what had taken him longer than anyone else to get there. "Oh, for godsakes–it *is* a leg."

"Sheriff, we call the coroner in for this?" Smoke asked.

Twardy frowned. "Good question, Detective. This is a first, as long as I've been with the department, all thirty-one years." He wiped the back of his hand across his brow. "Sergeant, phone Melberg and let him make the call. Tell him we'll start searching for the rest of her."

Dr. Gordon Melberg was the county coroner.

"Right." I stepped away from the others. Dr. Melberg answered on the third ring.

"Doc, it's Sergeant Aleckson. The sheriff asked me to call." I gave him a sumary of the dog's discovery.

Melberg clucked his tongue loudly against the roof of his mouth. "The M.E. is about finished here so I'll head up there shortly." He was observing an autopsy of a person who had allegedly stabbed himself, according to a witness. "Give me about an hour. Is the leg lying in the sun?"

"Yes, it is."

"Okay. Don't cover it, of course, but figure out a way to get some shade over it, protect it from the sun."

"Will do. Thanks, Doc."

I relayed Melberg's instructions to the others.

"Let's grab four of those stakes to build a little tent," Smoke directed.

Smoke, Mason, Carlson, and I each forced a stake into the ground a few feet from the leg to form four corners.

Smoke brushed his hands together. "Mason, got a tarp or blanket in the mobile unit?"

"Sure, I'll grab it."

We pulled the tarp over the stakes. Smoke looked up at the sky, then down at the leg. "Pull it a little more to the west to block out the sun." The four of us worked to make the adjustment. "We'll keep an eye on her, make sure we keep the sun off 'til Doc gets here."

11

We understood Smoke meant each one of us was responsible for that task.

Smoke jotted something on his memo pad. "We're going to need reinforcements to help with the search, keep the scene secure, interview neighbors."

The sheriff pulled out his phone. "I'll call the chief deputy to pull as many as he can. What'd think? Six more be enough?" he asked Smoke.

Smoke ran a hand across his chin. "Should be to get started. I'm thinkin' we'll need divers too, but I want to take a quick look-see around before we get 'em here."

The sheriff nodded and made his call.

"Okay, troops, let's get this roped off before anyone else shows up," Smoke advised.

"How much are you thinking, Detective?" Carlson asked.

"From here to the road, down the road the length of the lake." Smoke pointed out the areas in question. "If we spot tracks of a vehicle pulling off the road, go around 'em."

He paused a minute, scanning the lake and the land around it. From our north side vantage point, the east side was wooded and the south side had a gentle hill that rose perhaps five or six feet, then dropped into a swampy area. On the west, there was a fenced-in pasture on the other side of the road.

Todd Mason held the mobile unit's thirty-five millimeter camera. Smoke motioned to him.

"Start with the leg, then move down to the lake. When the homeowner comes back out we'll see where the dog found the leg. Hard to see from here, but it looks like there are a fair number of tracks by the water." He squinted and pointed to an area on the west bank.

"Aleckson and Carlson, you mark off the perimeter to the west there, then we'll take a closer look," Smoke instructed.

The house screen door closed and we turned to see Tara Engen coming toward us. Her drawn face had a little color restored to it and her shoulder length hair was wet and straight. Apparently she had done a quick shampoo and towel dry.

"Ms. Engen, you see where the dog found the leg?" Smoke asked.

Engen shook her head. "No. Zeke likes to go for a swim. He usually goes in over there." She waved her pointer finger in the direction where Smoke had noticed the tracks.

"It's easier to get in the lake, not so many weeds, like here." She indicated where her yard became swamp reeds and grasses by the lake. "Anyway, I was putzing around the yard, not paying much attention to him. On my way to the garden I heard Zeke barking, you know, like he was telling me something?" She searched Smoke's face and he nodded that he understood.

Engen exhaled sharply. "So I went back and saw Zeke had something laying on the ground. At first I thought it was a log, but it looked so weird. I couldn't figure out what it was for the longest time and Zeke just kept barking the whole time." Engen crossed her arms, resting them on her waist.

We were as still as four sculptures in Engen's garden, listening to her account, waiting for answers.

"Then what happened?" Smoke urged.

Engen closed her eyes and hugged herself tighter. "I think I screamed . . ." She paused, then nodded. "Yeah, I screamed. And that pretty much scared Zeke. He looked at me like he knew something awful had happened. I couldn't think of what to do next. Finally, I put Zeke in his kennel and called 911. Then I called my husband at work and told him to come home right away. He works in Plymouth and should be home any time now."

"You did exactly the right thing," the sheriff assured her.

Engen frowned. "Who would put a leg in our lake?"

The burning question.

"That's what we intend to find out," Smoke affirmed.

Sheriff Twardy took a step toward Engen and eased a reassuring hand on the back of her shoulder. "Let's go sit on your patio and let the deputies do their jobs."

Engen nodded and the sheriff ushered her away.

"We're going to need a bunch of stakes. Think we got enough?" I asked Brian Carlson.

"Should have." He was holding four or five. "We'll start marking and I'll grab more when we run out."

Carlson handed me the roll of crime scene tape, then stuck the first thin metal stake in the ground about eight feet north of where the leg lay. I attached the tape and unrolled as we walked toward the road, following the length of the Engen's driveway. Carlson and I kept our heads down, our eyes searching every inch of ground as we moved slowly along. Abbott Avenue ran anywhere between four and eight feet from Wolf Lake on the west side, following the shoreline. Carlson stuck a stake in the ground every eight feet, or so. I followed behind, attaching the tape.

2.

Langley Parker looked up from his microscope. He was alone in the lab. The other five researchers were on a coffee break or completing a task in another part of the building.

Langley preferred to spend his break time alone. He slid down in his chair, leaned his head back, and closed his eyes. Images, picture frame after picture frame, flashed before his mind's eye. The display speeded up to become a movie. Sound kicked in a moment later. Good memories were almost as enjoyable as the actual events. They could be brought to mind at will and savored over and over.

His smile faded. He'd think about personal pleasures later. Langley had important work he needed to concentrate on. He shook his head to loosen the distracting, pleasurable thoughts inveigling him.

The Veterinary Diagnostic Laboratory at the University of Minnesota, housed in a three-story brick building in St. Paul, was Langley's home away from home. The state-of-the-art laboratory was among the most advanced in the United States and served as the official laboratory of the Minnesota Board of Animal Health.

Langley had spent his weekdays, and sometimes his evenings, there for several years. The generous grant his stepfather gave the university helped secure a position for Langley as a laboratory geneticis, so he could pursue the one goal of his life: to find the cause of, and cure for, Equine Cerebellar Abiotrophy, or CA, a genetic, neurological condition found almost exclusively in Arabian horses. CA had killed Langley's first two horses and he owed it to Sheik, his extraordinary Arabian, to find the cure.

When Langley turned fourteen, his mother told him he would be "trusted" with the next Arabian foul born at their hobby farm. Langley would finally have someone to care for, someone to care about him. He researched horse names and decided if the horse was male, he would be named "Kemen", meaning "strong". If it was a female, she would be "Manda", or "battle maid".

Kemen it was—beautiful and perfect until he was two months old and began to have head tremors. He often lost his balance. His forelegs adopted a wide-based stance. He startled and fell easily. Although the veterinarian could not positively diagnose the condition, he surmised it was CA and suggested euthanasia. Langley's stepfather had no problem telling the vet to "take care of it."

Langley was secretly devastated. He mechanically told his parents he understood and they promised him the next foal. Manda showed symptoms of CA by six weeks. The same vet was called and "took care of it" again. Langley overheard his stepfather ask his mother if Langley was some sort of jinx.

Langley wondered the same thing.

He spent hours studying the horrifying disease which had taken his horses. He learned it was a genetic, neurological condition found almost exclusively in Arabian horses. Breeding experiments at a research facility showed a horse could carry the disease gene but not be affected by it. Breeding between two carrier horses produced an affected foal twenty-five percent of the time.

Langley learned the incidence of CA in Arabians wasn't known since there was no direct genetic test. Veterinarians could perform neurological tests to determine if symptoms were consistent with CA., but positive diagnosis was possible only through post-mortem examination.

He discovered the normal cerebellum of a horse was divided into two layers. The Purkinje cells were large neurons which lie on the border between them. The cells carried all the messages generated by the cerebellum and had control over movement and coordination.

In horses affected with CA, the Purkinje cells

began to degenerate and die soon after birth. The remaining Purkinje cells would atrophy and not regenerate. The animal would lose its sense of space and distance, making balance and coordination difficult—a dangerous condition for a horse.

"Okay, Langley, we're going to try one more time. I'm worried there must be something wrong with that new stallion we've got. We've never had trouble with our foals before," his stepfather had told him.

Langley worried for months about the expected foal. Finally, when he was sixteen, he got his very fine, very stately, very loyal Arabian: Sheik. His one true friend. His accomplice. The only one Langley trusted with his secrets. Sheik gave him the ability to concentrate, the will to get through his undergraduate and graduate programs.

But, more than that, Sheik gave him power. Riding on his back vanquished the impotence Langley had struggled with since childhood—feeling helpless, lonely, unloved. When Langley was on Sheik's back, galloping though the fields or walking through the woods, he felt powerful, in control and free. Langley became Gideon, "a warrior, one who cuts down."

Langley thought it was the greatest high in the world, until he discovered an even greater one: the ultimate dominance he had over his concubines.

3.

"Look at this–someone's been here on horseback," I noticed about halfway down the west side of Wolf Lake.

Carlson bent over and studied the ground. "Yeah, I'd say a single horse." He stood up and called out, "Dawes, Mason, we might have something here."

Carlson dropped the stakes he was holding on the ground and I laid the tape beside them. Smoke and Todd Mason took a break from their tasks and joined us. We all studied the hoof patterns.

"Looks like a guy was riding along and stopped here . . . the hoof prints follow down to the water. Probably letting the horse get a drink. On the other hand, could be to throw a leg in the lake," Smoke added.

I had been thinking the same thing. Mason and Carlson both nodded.

"A lot of people ride the trails in the park, Smoke. I saw a couple unloading horses from their trailer when I drove through yesterday," I said.

"It is a great place for riding," Mason said.

"Ever take a cast of horse hoof impressions?" Smoke asked.

"Nope." Carlson and Mason agreed, shaking their heads.

"It'll be a new one for you, then." Smoke got down on his hands and knees and perused the prints. "You're the farm kid, Corky. These hoof prints tell you anything?"

"About the horse?" I studied for a moment. "Well, it was barefoot, meaning it didn't have horseshoes on. These ridges are most likely 'grass rings' because they run all the way around the foot." I waved my hand over the hoof pattern.

"What does that mean?" Smoke asked.

"That the horse is pastured, and when there are

changes in the weather conditions–you know, moisture followed by periods of dryness in the pasture–they develop. Temperature changes are another cause. They're pretty common. Oh, and it also happens when there is exercise followed by little activity for a while."

Smoke crawled backward a few steps then jumped to his feet. "And what does that tell us?"

I shrugged. "The owner keeps his horse in a pasture in Minnesota where the weather fluctuates from hot to cold, wet to dry."

"Like the rings on a tree? You can tell what the weather was like by how thick the ring is?" Mason asked.

"Not quite."

"Back to our horse and rider," Smoke directed.

"Maybe the guy has a busy schedule and rides the horse when he can," I offered, shaking my head. "I'm not an expert on horse hooves. Oh look, there's a crack on the right front hoof."

The three officers drew closer to me as I pointed out the flaw.

"What's that from?" Carlson wondered.

"Maybe a harder ride some time–got a little injury. A farrier could fix it. I'm thinking the horse is most likely pastured and probably not ridden a lot."

"So not a horse from one of the riding stables?" Smoke asked.

"No, they'd have shoes on their horses."

"So why would a guy not shoe his horse?" Mason asked.

"It's not the way nature intended, I guess. Shoes can cause lots of problems. Like, they restrict blood flow to the hooves and interfere with the natural expansion and contraction of the hoof when it's weight-bearing. Plus, the nails driven into the hooves leave holes and weakened areas."

The sheriff joined us. Engen still sat–more like slouched in a lawn chair on her patio.

"What'd ya got going here?" Twardy asked.

As Smoke explained, I walked down the road

about eight feet then headed back, examining the prints. I paused where the horse had stopped by the lake.

"Hmm. Okay guys, this is interesting. C'mere." I waved them to follow me.

"We have a rider going down the gravel road. Not much for impressions where the gravel is packed hard, but here, more on the shoulder, the impressions are deeper."

The team stayed close. "Then we get to the spot . . . here . . . where the horse goes to the water's edge, stands there for I don't know how long, then backs up, turns around and . . ." I led the others as we followed the prints across the road and back south again for a few feet.

"Damn," Smoke said.

"You got it. The horse was carrying a heavier load before it stopped then it was after it got going again."

"So that kinda backs up my gut feeling there is more of our victim in the lake than that one leg we got lying over there." Smoke took in a big inhale and blew out the air slowly, one of the things he did when he was pondering something.

"What do you figure the horse weighs, any guesstimates?" The sheriff directed his question to me.

"That's all it would be is a guesstimate."

I paced off the distance from the front and hind legs when the horse was in a standing position. "I would say the horse is about . . . five feet . . . in length . . . fourteen to sixteen hands . . . around a thousand pounds. With a rider, maybe twelve-hundred. The impressions are fairly deep, but not excessively so."

The sheriff had been part of the Winnebago County Mounted Patrol Unit and most likely knew more about horses than any of us, but he kept that to himself. Sheriff Twardy was a unique leader. He showed up at all the major crime scenes—he said it was too much in his blood not to be there—but he mainly observed and rarely gave any directions or orders. He trusted his officers to conduct the investigations and come to conclusions based on what they found.

"Yeah, I'd say a thousand, give or take, is about right," Smoke agreed. "Sheriff?"

The sheriff considered and nodded.

Smoke rubbed his jaw. "What'd you suppose that leg weighs? What, fifteen, twenty pounds?"

I shrugged and said, "Maybe." I discreetly lifted my right leg slightly and tried to guess its weight, something that had never occurred to me to consider until that very minute.

No one else commented, but they appeared deep in thought.

"Twenty pounds wouldn't add much weight, but, say one hundred-thirty, forty, fifty pounds would be enough to explain the deeper depressions." Smoke squatted for another close check. "We'll send the impressions to the BCA for their expert opinion, but that'd be mine, if I had to give it."

He stood up and stuck his reading glasses in his pocket. "Mason, Carlson, finish marking off the scene and get it photographed. Aleckson, we'll follow these hoof prints, see where they lead to."

"You want underwater recovery started?" Mason asked.

"You're part of that, right?" Smoke said.

"Yup. So's Carlson."

"You got your gear with?"

Mason nodded. "We threw it in the unit when we heard 'lake.'"

"Good. Yeah, why don't you give Warner a holler. Tell him to load up the boat and assemble the rest of his team. We should have this much processed before the whole place is crawling with deputies. Corky, let's take that walk. Why don't you grab your camera?"

Carlson picked up the crime scene tape and stakes and handed the tape to Mason. He helped Carlson finish the job I had started, continuing to the south side of the lake where the shoreline turned east and the road continued south. The sheriff moved to the outside of the

21

marked area.

I found a camera in its case in my trunk, pulled the attached strap around my neck, and caught up with Smoke.

A newer gray Toyota made its way toward us at a fairly fast clip, then slowed when it got closer. The man in the vehicle raised and lowered his hand in a quick wave of acknowledgement and pulled into the Engen's driveway. He got out of the car and Tara was in his arms a second later.

"Good." Smoke gave me a relieved nod. "Let's move."

We walked south on Abbott Avenue to Eighty-fifth Street and started to turn left. I glanced back to see Mason taking pictures of the horse hoof prints and Carlson writing in a pocket notebook. The sheriff had his arms crossed on his chest, watching them work.

"Wait a minute." Smoke stopped and pointed. "The prints are coming and going both directions. Let's head west first." We walked about one hundred yards to the edge of a small swamp where the horse and rider had been.

"I sure hope this doesn't mean there's another body part in this swamp," I said.

"Doesn't look good, does it? Better snap some photos of these, in case."

"The prints look like they came from the direction of the park–rode to the swamp here–turned around and headed up Abbott to Wolf." I narrated as I took the pictures.

"I guess we'll find out if that means anything when underwater goes into Wolf. If we don't find the rest of her in there, this is going to turn into an even bigger nightmare than it already is. We got about four hours of daylight left–a little less. Let's head east." Smoke pointed to where the road ended and the grassy area began. "Looks like he stayed on the road for a while, then headed into the park here."

"Smoke, a horse could have traveled for miles," I

protested, snapping more shots.

"Yeah, I basically wanted to see if he came from the park. I'll have boat and water load up the four-wheeler—"

I interrupted. "Maybe a mounted patrol would be better—could go where the other horse did. It'd be easier for the rider to see than from a four-wheeler."

Smoke smiled and tapped me on the back. "Now you're thinkin'. We'll head back and I'll call in the reinforcements." He opened his phone and hit two digits on speed dial.

"Robin? . . . Yes, it *is* a real leg . . . Young, twenties, thirties . . . Horrible is one word for it . . . Underwater's already been called, you should hear them rolling any minute. What I need is one mounted. Who's on call? . . . Called in sick? Okay, well who's next on the list? . . . Good. Get him out here, a-sap."

By the time Smoke clapped his phone shut, we were back on Abbott.

"What would possess someone to cut somebody up?" I asked, hypothetically.

I had some knowledge on the psychology of why.

"Very, very sick people are possessed in the most bizarre ways. Has to be the first dismemberment case in the county's history—that I know of anyway. The sheriff said it's the first in his thirty-one years."

"Makes Alvie Eisner look a little less crazy," I thought out loud.

"Yeah, right." Sarcasm oozed through his words. "Don't go down that road or you'll drive yourself crazy trying to figure out the motivations of society's sickos.

"'*Vice is a monster of frightful mien*
As to be hated needs but to be seen
Yet seen too oft, familiar with her face
We first endure, then pity, then embrace.'"

I stopped to watch Smoke during his recitation. "Okay! Where did that come from?"

"'An Essay on Man' by Alexander Pope, English poet, late 1700s. We read him in a college English class I took about a hundred years ago. For some reason, those lines stuck with me."

"Alexander Pope? The name is familiar, but—"

"You've heard him quoted a lot. He's the guy who wrote 'a little learning is a dangerous thing', 'to err is human, to forgive, divine', 'fools rush in where angels fear to tread', 'hope springs eternal.'"

I smiled and nodded. "Oh, he's the guy? Well, thank you, Professor Dawes."

Smoke bent over slightly in a mock bow. "Any time. Change of subject: since you brought up our least favorite inmate—let me reiterate—I do *not* want you seeing Eisner. Period. She had her chance to spill her guts. You are not at her beck and call, little lady." Smoke hit the palm of his hand with the opposite fist. "My insides turn over every time I remember how you looked after your fight with that monster."

"All right, Detective. We both know we're not going to settle this today. Let's talk about it later."

"Yeah." Smoke studied the lake, obviously thinking about the secrets it may be holding. "What we got going here is priority one."

On that we could wholeheartedly agree.

4.

Driving to his apartment after a long day at the lab, Langley longed to relive his latest conquest. Instead, life at his grandparents' farm sprang unbidden from the his memory. Every weekend, from his earliest recollection until he was sixteen, his mother left him there so she could spend her time as she pleased, unburdened by the responsibilities of motherhood. Langley's mouth turned down in disgust.

At age seven, he was about to enter the kitchen when he heard his grandparents talking about him. He hung back in the doorway to watch and listen.

"What do you expect? What was his mother thinking when she named him 'Langley'? How can the poor boy grow up normal with a name like that?" Grandmother asked Grandfather.

"Mother, Naomi just has some high-falutin' ideas, is all. She likes fancy things and Langley is kind of a fancy name."

"All those years of you spoiling Naomi, putting big ideas in her head. First, she marries a doctor, then the CEO of a big company. She thinks she can just run off and play every weekend and leave her son with us. We're too old to be raising the boy. That should be up to his mother."

Grandmother wrung her kitchen towel. "And, if that's not bad enough, she needs to tell the boy about his father and baby sister. He deserves to know they're waiting for him in heaven."

"Everyone grieves in their own way. Naomi just couldn't come to grips after the accident like other folks can." Grandfather folded his hands and clicked his thumbs.

"Well, the Lord spared her and the boy for a reason. It was a terrible thing losing Ken and little Arielle,

but she still had the boy. To up and marry Ken's best friend, not one year later, just didn't leave her time to grieve, proper-like."

He must have moved enough to get Grandmother's attention.

"Langley! What are you doing standing in the doorway? You eavesdropping?"

He didn't know what eavesdropping was, but the way Grandmother said it, it didn't sound like a good thing to do. He had no answer.

His grandmother leaned her face close to his. "Were you listening to what me and your grandfather were saying?"

"Yes, ma'am."

"Did you understand what we were talking about?"

"Yes ma'am."

He had a father and sister waiting for him in heaven.

His mother had high-falutin' ideas.

His grandparents were too old to raise him.

The man he called "Daddy" was not his father.

His grandmother didn't think his name was "normal." What was normal?

Grandmother threw the dishtowel on the counter and crossed her arms. "All right, then. We won't speak of it again, but you tell your mother what you heard and ask her to tell you more about it. Understood?"

"Yes ma'am."

"Let's get some food into that stomach of yours."

True to her word, his grandmother never spoke of his father and sister again. Not true to his, Langley never asked his mother about them. Instead, he tore a sheet of paper from his grandmother's tablet and wrote down the name Ken and a seven-year-old's spelling of Arielle. He set about snooping through his mother's things whenever possible. There was nothing under her bed or in her closet. He finally uncovered two boxes in a spare bedroom. One box was filled with baby girl clothes, a pink *knitted blanket, a silver cup engraved with "Arielle", a framed picture of a blue-eyed baby girl–under a year old– and a few small toys.*

In the second box, the first thing he found was a man's wallet. Langley opened it and pulled out a driver's license with the name Kenneth Peter Dietz. Kenneth Peter Dietz. Brown hair and green eyes, same as Langley's.

A folded newspaper article tucked under the wallet revealed details of the crash. "Dr. Kenneth Dietz, age 29, of Hamel and his infant daughter, Arielle, died in a motor vehicle accident Saturday. Dr. Dietz pulled onto Highway 55 and was struck by a pickup truck driven by Sherman Crawley. Other passengers in the Dietz vehicle, Naomi Dietz, age 24 and Langley, age 3, were taken to the hospital, treated, and released. Crawley was not injured. All the adults were wearing seatbelts and the children were in child restraint seats."

Langley put everything back in the boxes. Dietz. His real name was Dietz. Why would his mother take that away from him, along with any memories of the man who gave it to him?

His sister? She was probably better off. His mother didn't have much time for kids.

He carried the surname Dietz as his own secret. When he got older and rode his Arabian, he found he needed a first name to match the power and might he had gained. That's when he discovered the name Gideon. He would become the warrior, the one who cut down. Gideon Dietz.

Work was the one thing his grandparents understood and they thrived on it. Langley learned, early on, how to feed the chickens and gather eggs and slop the pigs and spread hay in the barn. He hated the smell of chickens, sheep, pigs, and cows. He hated the smell of every farm animal except horses—he found their strangely sour smell pleasant.

He would sneak into the horse barn with his

grandfather's Belgians to inhale their scent. Langley associated their distinctive odor with strength, might, forcefulness. They were certainly more powerful than his aging grandparents; even more powerful than his mother and the man he had believed was his father.

The sheer strength of the horses encouraged Langley, gave him mettle. After spending time with them, Langley felt brave enough to tell his grandfather "no" to certain chores. His grandfather would turn him over to his grandmother for discipline.

"Mother, Langley refuses to slop the pigs." Or, "Mother, Langley will not help me clean the chicken coop." Or, "Mother, the boy says he won't milk the cows."

Each infraction necessitated Grandmother's own special brand of discipline. She made Langley sit in a corner of the living room and read the Bible so he could reflect on the error of his ways. Langley couldn't fake it, either. His grandmother would quiz him on what he read and what it meant. Some of the stories were interesting, but he didn't really understand their meaning.

When Langley was thirteen he found an unforgettable story in the Old Testament Book of Judges, chapter nineteen. He read it three times. When his grandmother asked about his reading, Langley recited one he had read some weeks earlier. He did not want to share the story of the concubine with his grandmother, or anyone else.

He kept it to himself, pondered it, savored it.

It became his personal obsession.

5.

Carlson poured plaster of paris in the four best hoof prints, one for each separate hoof. On and off duty deputies arrived, either ready for assignment or to satisfy their natural, albeit morbid, curiosities. Most everyone paraded over to gaze at the tent-protected leg as the first order of business.

Smoke waved at the incoming vehicles to park on the west side of Abbott Avenue. Deputies gathered close along the band of crime scene tape.

"Listen up! Before we completely implode here, the first thing I want everyone to do is sign in. Sergeant Aleckson, start a sheet."

I left to grab a crime scene sign-in form from my squad car. Every officer there could be required to write a report, if need be. I listened to Smoke's instructions all the way to my car and back again.

"I don't have to tell you how to conduct yourselves at this scene. We've got a lot of ground—and water—to cover in a few short hours. How many divers we got here?"

Each one sounded off.

"Weber."

"Carlson."

"Roth."

"Mason."

"Okay. Weber, Carlson, and Mason, suit up. Sergeant Roth, I need you to help with some interviews. If we need you in the water later, we'll pull you then."

I returned with the form secured to a clipboard, jotted the date and location then handed it to the sheriff who passed it to the next guy who passed it on until it came back to me.

Warner pulled up with the boat trailer in tow, stuck his head out his open window, and pushed his sunglasses to the top of his head. "Where do you want me?"

Smoke indicated his head to the right. "Park in the driveway, for now. If you go in, it'll be on the north side, there. Any idea how deep this lake is?"

"I got a rough idea–not deep. I'll grab my county lake book, the depths are detailed in it."

Smoke's lips turned up in a smirk. "So Wolf's big enough to qualify as a lake?"

"Yeah, not much bigger than a pond, is it?" Warner smiled and scratched his arm.

"Our guys will be more like walkers than divers." Smoke raised his eyebrows.

Warner nodded. "Just as well. The water's a little on the murky side."

Weber was the stockiest of the divers and the last to emerge from the crime lab, which served as a dressing room. Three wet suits with face masks, head lamps, fins, and breathing apparatus were ready. Other deputies hovered nearby, waiting for assignments. Smoke pulled out his notepad and pen. His readers rested on the end of his nose and he peered over them to pick out deputies.

"Norwood and Ortiz: it'll be up to you to keep the scene secure. There's not a load of traffic on this road, but this time of the day, with people coming home from work, could be more than we'd figure. And *no* civilian goes near that leg.

"Roth, Holman, Levasseur, Pickering: you'll canvass the area. Interview all the neighbors within a two mile radius. Doesn't have to be real in-depth. Did they see or hear anything suspicious–a guy on horseback, someone going through with a horse trailer–the last couple of days?

"There're more houses to the west so you can divide those up.

"Aleckson and Zubinski: interview the Engens, separately. Maybe something unusual they saw or heard will shake loose from their brains."

Warner handed his lake book to Smoke.

"Divers, let's take a look at this map. It's only

about two feet deep at the shore, deepest part is more toward the south end–twenty-four feet there. Otherwise, straight out from here, it's about eighteen feet in the middle. Go in on your stomachs, arm's length apart out from the hoof prints. All right, everybody, let's do it!" Smoke clapped his hands.

"Aleckson, Zubinski. The A to Z team, huh?" Carlson teased when we met on the way to our assignments.

I rolled my eyes. "Not funny." Those closest to me in the department knew Mandy Zubinski was my least favorite deputy. She had started a rumor about Smoke and me having an affair the previous year. Most of my colleagues thought it was because she was interested in Smoke and jealous of the easy relationship I shared with him. I tried not to be bothered by gossip, but sometimes I had trouble letting it slide off my back.

The divers stirred up the layers of silt which had settled on the bottom of the small lake from years of soil run-off. Particles of dirt rose to the surface and covered them as they crawled into the lake on their bellies.

Zubinski caught up to me halfway up the Engen's driveway. "Who do you want me to interview, Sergeant?"

"You take Mrs. I'll take Mr."

6.

Langley fought his urges for years. Riding Sheik soothed him until the day he saw her on Hennepin Avenue, inviting him. Blonde hair, blue eyes. Inviting him. So easy. It was his first time with a woman and he knew just what he wanted to do. He had fantasized far too long. It had been building in him forever and it was time to act. He was ready and had prepared well.

She went home with him to his top floor warehouse apartment. He hadn't originally planned to keep her for three days; he just couldn't let her go. He held her one more day and indulged himself until the end was inevitable. The greater she suffered, the more fulfilled he felt. Langley was in complete control of his concubine, invigorated, alive. Everything about his time with the one he called "Eve" had been perfect.

Langley slipped a disc into his DVD player, settled on a chair close to the screen, and pushed "play." Every nerve, muscle, and brain cell jumped with anticipation. The hours he spent with his concubine were recorded for posterity and his personal viewing pleasure.

Whether she was gagged and tied to the chair or lying on the bed with her legs and arms cuffed to the four corners, Langley had complete dominion over her. She was evil and it was up to him to take her power away. His video camera captured each panicked expression, every futile pleading look, and grimaces of pain. By the second day her pain, her suffering, her fear was reaching the climax. By the third day, when he clutched his teeth into her thigh, it was complete. Her eyes revealed her surrender. She had given up; she was nothing.

It was time.

Her struggle for air as his fingers dug into her neck prompted Langley to plunge them deeper still, until life fled from her eyes and her body stilled. And then, the ultimate release: he used his power saw to divide her into six pieces of less than nothing.

The final triumph.

The Levite in the book of Judges divided his concubine into twelve pieces and sent them into areas of Israel as a message, but Langley didn't want to send out a public message. The six pieces were for his grandmother, grandfather, mother, father, sister, and himself. His stepfather didn't count. Five pieces to be delivered to places that had haunted him since childhood. The places he suffered private torture. Five pieces, as unknown and unseen offerings, for the people who had neglected and berated him, and the best piece for himself, to keep and to savor.

It was personal. Very, very personal.

He placed the concubine's torso in a garbage bag, and the garbage bag into a large gym bag. Her arms and legs went in another. Sixty pounds or so, in each hand, wasn't too much for him to tote. Her head went into his freezer so he could have a look whenever he desired.

It was nearly midnight when Langley drove with the remains to his mother's and stepfather's farm. No one used the private lake on their property–a perfect burial site. No one would ever find what was left of Langley's first concubine.

7.

Zubinski finished her interview with Mrs. Engen before I was through interviewing Mr. Engen. She leaned against the sheriff's car, jotting notes in her memo pad.

"Anything?" I asked, momentarily taken by the way her coppery hair became fingers of fire in the sun.

I reluctantly admitted she had very striking hair.

Zubinski looked up. "Nah. Tara said they bought the place from an older couple just over a year ago. They moved out from the Twin Cities–liked the setting, old farmhouse, outbuildings. Hope to get horses, chickens, etc., soon. They've been working on the house, light remodeling. Wanted to get that done first. They haven't met many of the neighbors.

"Said she works part-time as a hospice nurse. Her husband commutes to Plymouth. She didn't see anything, hear anything unusual. She's never been in the lake. No swimming or lake sports. I'd say she never will be either, after this." Zubinski nodded at the leg and scrunched up her face.

I took another peek at the leg under its tent. "Well, their stories corroborate. Dean Engen is a financial planner. They like the setting of the lake and he's done a little casting from shore, but says the bass in there are muddy tasting, not very edible."

I looked at Zubinski and shrugged. "That seems to be the extent of their lake activities." I jotted Engen's full name and date of birth on a memo sheet and handed it to her. "Here's his info. Run a check on them. Since they've both been backgrounded for their jobs, I have a feeling there won't be anything, but never say never, right?"

Mandy nodded and headed to her squad car.

Dr. Gordon Melberg pulled into the driveway. He got out of his car, stretched his legs, then jogged over to the tent-protected leg. I followed close behind.

"My, my, my. Not a good way to start the week at all." The creases by his eyes deepened in a squint.

"Or end it," I said.

"That would be more accurate, certainly, as far as our victim was concerned." Melberg pulled on two pairs of latex gloves and squatted by the leg. His muscular legs and arms strained against his clothes. "Very clean cut. Post-mortem. It couldn't have been in the water long. No adipocere—"

"No what?"

He glanced up at me and pronounced it more distinctly. "Adipocere."

"Oh, grave wax?"

Melberg's attention went back to the leg. "Correct. It's a water-insoluble material consisting mostly of saturated fatty acids. It's formed by the slow hydrolysis of fats in the decomposing body by anaerobic bacteria. A cold and humid environment without oxygen speeds up the formation of adipocere. The inches of muddy sediment at the bottom of this lake would be ideal to form the matter."

"Doc." Sheriff Twardy and Smoke joined us at the tent.

"Sheriff, Detective."

"Divers got in the water a few minutes ago. Least it's a small lake," the sheriff said.

"Not much more than a pond," Smoke added.

The sheriff frowned, taking another look at the leg. "Any idea how long she's been in the water?"

"I was just telling the sergeant—not long. Skin's intact, no adipocere. If we find the rest of her, her vital organs will give us more accurate information." Melberg pressed slightly on the thigh then quickly released his fingers.

Smoke pointed to a mark. "That bite before or after she died?"

"Boforo."

"Oh, for godsakes," the sheriff muttered.

Weber popped up from underwater, pulled off his

oxygen mask, and yelled, "Sheriff! We got something."

The four of us jogged to the shoreline and deputies filled in around us.

The other two divers surfaced about eight feet out.

"Something's in here." Weber hoisted a garbage bag to the surface and Carlson put his hands under the load to help Weber walk it to the shore.

The bag was made of heavy duty plastic and the open end was tied together. When Weber and Carlson lifted it out of the lake, water ran from multiple small holes. An upside down water fountain, like my grandmother's old-fashioned sprinkling can.

"Well, we know why it sank," Smoke concluded.

As the water drained out, the black bag took on the form of a woman's torso, shoulders, breasts, stomach.

"Someone grab a blanket to lay this on," Smoke directed.

"I got it." Zubinski was back a moment later.

"This looks like the most level spot." Smoke pointed to a spot not far from the hoof prints. Mandy shook out the gray wool blanket and laid it on the ground.

"Okay, guys, put her down." Smoke snapped on gloves while Weber and Carlson slowly lowered their package to the blanket-covered ground.

No one uttered a word as we all fixated on the plastic-clad form. I reached into the glove pouch on my belt and struggled to pull a pair of latex gloves onto my sweating hands. I noticed others had the same problem.

"Detective?" Melberg prompted.

Smoke glanced at the doctor. "Aside from the obvious, my concern is preserving possible evidence on the bag. Flashlight, anyone?"

I handed mine over.

Smoke knelt beside the form, tipping his head to the side, his eyes following the streams of light to the bag. "I don't see any prints, but there could be some in the folds, or inside, or hidden somewhere. Sergeant, can you cut the bag open on the bottom seam, there? I don't want to disturb the tied end."

I pulled out my jackknife, opened it, and painstakingly sliced the straightest line possible, to open the bag. I held my breath against the assaulting odor of wet, decaying flesh.

"Okay, everyone gloved up?" Smoke glanced at the sheriff, Melberg, Zubinski, and me. "Sheriff, Zubinski, I want you to get on either side of the bag. Use the thumb and pointer of each hand and carefully grasp the top of the bag with one hand and the bottom with the other."

They knelt on opposite sides of the blanket and followed Smoke's instruction. "Got it?"

They both nodded.

"Now pull the top taut."

They did.

"Okay, Corky, cut the bag open, right down the middle."

I crouched on the blanket next to Mandy, aimed my knife up so it would stay as far away from the object in the bag as possible, and sliced the plastic.

I thought I was prepared, but how could I be? There was a collective, audibly loud and sharp gasp from eight professionals–people used to gory sights–sharing the mutual shock of seeing a headless, limbless torso.

Mandy turned her face away from me and started coughing into her shoulder. I managed to hold my breath instead.

"In all my years . . ." The sheriff rubbed his cheeks with both hands.

Dr. Melberg withdrew a thermometer from his back pocket. He inserted it into a spot on the lower right side of the torso. We watched as the mercury rose to seventy-five degrees Fahrenheit.

"That's a surprise. Internal temp is seventy-five degrees. The water temp is seventy-two–hasn't even gotten down to that yet." Melberg looked directly at the sheriff. "She's been dead no more than twenty-four hours. Probably got here sometime last night." He stood, pulled off his gloves then jotted the data on his notepad.

Smoke stared at the torso and shook his head.

"Corky, since I pulled the crime lab guys out to dive, you get the pictures. Zubinski, log what she snaps."

"Yes, sir." Zubinski had finally stopped coughing.

I was relieved to step away from the scene for the time it took to retrieve my camera from the hood of my car. I glanced at Ortiz and Norwood who were keeping the perimeter secure, beyond curious to see what the divers had landed. Tara and Dean Engen rose from their chairs, straining to get a glimpse from a distance while keeping their feet planted as firmly as the flowers around the patio.

My brain was not quite able to translate what had occurred at Wolf Lake into real events. A woman's leg rested on a lawn under a makeshift tent and her torso lay on layers of plastic and wool not far away.

"–if there's any more." I caught the last few words of Smoke's sentence.

"Let's do it," Carlson said and the divers pulled on their masks for round two.

I had helped my mother clothe the mannequins at her dress shop a number of times. As a young child, I found the lifeless forms frightening. Their eyes gazed off in the distance, but if I looked long enough, I imagined them moving slightly, watching me. When the shop door opened, or if a person walked by the adult-size dolls, their clothes would stir, giving them the appearance of being alive, breathing, shifting.

"Corky? You okay?" Smoke leaned closer.

"Oh, yeah, sure."

But mannequins didn't have belly buttons or rib bones or nipples or blood vessels or skin with freckles and moles. I snapped one photo after the next from various angles, wondering if the young woman had any clue what would become of her. Did her killer talk to her, say anything as he tortured her, or did he just let her imagination come to its own conclusions?

"More bite marks." Melberg's voice was strained. "Those two inches of the neck show evidence of strangulation. Looks like the leg belongs here." He pointed to the groin area where the leg had been severed.

"I hate him, whoever did this to her!" Mandy drove her pen into her notepad a few times.

No one disputed her words.

Smoke got a phone call from Deputy Griffin, the mounted patrol officer. He hung up and reported. "Griffin's going to unload the horse in the park, then head this way to begin tracking."

Mason surfaced with another loaded garbage bag. Water streamed from a large gash in the bottom. He walked to shore holding the package as far away from his body as his arms would allow. Carlson stood up, waist high in the water, with what I quickly identified as an arm.

"Might as well flip it so the tear is on the top. Let's lay it on the blanket." Smoke reached out to help Mason negotiate the bag and its contents. They lowered it to the ground.

Smoke glanced at the camera in my hand. "Zubinski, you can make the slice on this one. Sheriff, if you'll take that side, I'll take this one." They held the bag away from what was inside as Zubinski cut it open.

Another leg and another arm.

"I think the bag caught on a sharp rock. That must be how the first leg fell out," Mason said.

"She's starting to come together," Melberg quipped.

Professionals who deal with death on a regular basis say unexpected things and often have unusual senses of humor.

"Least now we got fingerprints," Smoke added.

Carlson, still holding the other arm, waited impatiently for instructions. When Melberg relieved him of his load, Carlson waved me over and pointed to his mask. I lifted it away from his face.

"I am going to burn these gloves."

"I'm getting a whole new wet suit," Mason said.

Carlson nodded. "Not a bad idea."

"Where's her head? Think it fell out, too?" Smoke asked.

Mason shrugged. "We didn't find it, but it sure could be in there somewhere, I guess."

Suddenly, the small lake looked mammoth with a myriad of hiding spots.

Griffin rode past our group, seated on his American Quarter Horse. He waved, turned around, and continued slowly back into the park.

Deputy Warner moved in next to Smoke. "If the divers don't locate the head in the next, say thirty minutes, I'll launch the boat. The sonar system should find it."

"Be nice to have one of those remote operated vehicles, Sheriff, like St. Louis County has," Smoke said.

Warner smiled.

"Be nice to have a lot of things, keep up with all the latest technology," the sheriff agreed.

Smoke lifted his hand in my direction. "Corky, you get the best fingerprints of anyone here. Grab the portable kit from the lab. I'll hold her arms, you roll."

I had never taken fingerprints from a dead body before, much less from detached arms. My hands were shaking when I began my task. Smoke held her right arm, then her left, as I inked each finger and rolled each one on the card.

Smoke's lopsided grin deepened his left dimple. "I was wondering how you'd do with those trembling fingers of yours, but you somehow managed to get clean, readable prints."

"Yeah, thanks." I pulled off my gloves and wiped my damp hands on my pants.

My eyes met Zubinski's. There was no evident envy or gloating. It was the first time in our two years working together I caught a hint of admiration on her face.

The mounted officer returned with news. "I followed the tracks to the parking area on the west side of the park, there. Looks like he drove an SUV, pulling a two-wheel trailer. There are footprints and tire marks, nothing very distinct, not enough to cast, but I got pictures."

Neither the divers, nor Warner and his sonar system, were able to locate the victim's head.

The three divers formed a semi-circle in front of Smoke. "You guys have already put a lot of time and effort into this, but I think we need to check one more location."

Weber sucked in a breath. "Where's that?"

Smoke pointed to the swamp where the horse had gone first. "Can you handle another hour or so?"

"Swamp's too shallow to put the boat in," Warner noted.

Mason's lips turned up in a slight grin. "That's why we get paid the big bucks."

Warner and the dive team headed to the swamp.

Melberg turned to the sheriff and Smoke. "We need to call the mortician to transport our victim to Hennepin; get her in the morgue as soon as possible, ready for autopsy."

"Thanks, Doc, you're right. The closest one is Little Mountain?" Smoke asked.

He nodded. "Yes. I'll call them."

The two directors/owners of McKay and Hall's Funeral Chapel arrived a short time later in their white transport van. Apparently, they thought it was not the kind of job to pass on to their employees who normally picked up bodies of the deceased.

Both men were in their fifties and it was the first time I had seen either one of them in casual clothing. I always assumed the first thing they did in the morning was put on their suits and ties, and the last thing they did before climbing into bed was to take them off. I guess I was wrong.

McKay, the shorter and balder of the two, talked to Melberg while Hall pulled a stretcher out of the vehicle and laid a body bag on top. He unzipped the bag then joined his partner and the doctor by the body.

Melberg pointed to Engen's front yard. "Her other leg is over there, under that tent. We're still looking for her head. When, and if, we recover that, I'll personally take it down to Hennepin."

"They know we're coming?" McKay asked.

Melberg swatted at a mosquito. "I talked to the M.E. a while ago to alert him. I'll call again when you're on your way."

McKay and Hall left with Ms. Doe's recovered body parts and the necessary paperwork. The divers continued to hunt for her head. At dusk, after painstaking hours in the water, the search was called. The evening air cooled as the sun lowered and a gentle breeze stirred, raising goose bumps on my sweaty arms. More mosquitoes found their way out of their daytime shelters and buzzed around us.

"Gather round!" Smoke called.

The deputies moved in. Mason, Carlson, and Weber were weary and worn. It had been a trying few hours for everyone on the scene.

Sheriff Twardy put his hand on Smoke's shoulder. "Well done, Detective, and thanks to all of you. It was a tough day and you made me proud of your professional conduct. Detective?"

Smoke scanned our faces. "I'll second that. Thanks, Sheriff. We're essentially done with the scene here. Let's get everything cleaned up. Aleckson, you're in charge of the evidence–the garbage bags, the casts of the hoof prints, the photos, the fingerprints. You're scheduled for evenings tomorrow?"

"Yes."

He nodded. "You too, Zubinski?"

"Yes, sir."

"Sheriff, can we get their shifts covered? I want them to take the evidence to the Bureau of Criminal Apprehension first thing in the morning. I got court, otherwise I'd go."

Twardy nodded. "I'll call Chief Deputy Kenner to take care of it."

I shot Smoke a "do you have to saddle me with Zubinski?" look but he chose to ignore it.

"Okay, Aleckson, Zubinski, I want you down there by 0900. I'll talk to my friend Darin. He'll be expecting

you, unless you hear different. Bags, casts, fingerprints."
Smoke raised his voice to be heard above the rising din.
"Anyone who took photos–get them into evidence, a-sap.
Let's finish up here. Oh, and one other thing. I'm going to
arrange a de-briefing, sooner rather than later. I don't
think any of us realizes how hard this might hit."

8.

Langley ejected the first DVD and loaded the second one marked "Eve II." She was nearly identical to Eve I in looks. He had done very well to find her out of all the harlots walking the streets of Minneapolis. If Langley and either one of the Eves had walked into a room together, people would remark on what a handsome couple they made. Eve was beautiful. That's what made her so dangerous.

He gave very little thought to his own looks. Once a week he trimmed his beard. That was about as much time as he spent on his own reflection. In college, girls would give him "looks." Langley knew the young women were dangerous and he knew what they wanted. But he couldn't be distracted from his number one priority: getting through his studies so he could find the cure for CA. Sheik came first. His urges and plans would come to fruition in due time.

Langley grew the beard to hide his face, and himself, from the world and its women.

He focused on the DVD. Eve II closed her eyes more than Eve I had, but her pain–her suffering–was just as great and almost as exciting. Three days of inflicting the payback she deserved. When it was time, Langley pressed his hands into her neck until life left those blue eyes forever. He placed her on his sturdy, plastic-covered table and set to work with his saw, dividing her into six pieces.

Langley turned off the television when the DVD ended. His memory picked up where his video taping left off.

Burying Eve II took more guts than burying Eve I, and was more dangerous. Langley had to leave her in Wolf Lake where he had first read about the Levite and his concubine. It was the place he spent every weekend *growing up. The place he learned the joy horses brought him. The place he felt almost as unloved as he did at his parents' house.*

Eve II was a little lighter than Eve I. Langley's apartment was on the third and top floor of the converted warehouse. Half of the six spaces were vacant and he rarely saw any of the other occupants. He made his way down the elevator and out to where his vehicles were parked. He cruised for Eves in his tan Chevy Malibu. His mother had given him the new silver Lexus Coupe, a sleek, hard-top convertible to replace his older car. But Langley felt safer, less noticeable in the Malibu. He knew he would never drive with the top down on the Lexus, so the convertible feature was wasted on him.

It was nearly eight o'clock and the sun would be setting soon. He had a two hour window to get to Lake Pearl State Park, deliver Eve to her final resting place, and get out of the park before the ten o'clock closing time.

He made the drive to Hamel following all traffic laws to the letter, defensively watching other vehicles for sudden moves that could cause a crash. At his parents' farm, Langley moved Eve to the back of his stepfather's Ford Expedition SUV and hitched up the horse trailer. Sheik was excited to see him and whinnied when Langley threw on his saddle and bridle and led him into the trailer.

They were going to the country for a ride.

"I'll tell you all about it when we get you back home. I just don't have enough time right now," he murmured to the sleek animal.

Langley made the drive in record time. He entered the park on the east side and drove past a few vehicles parked here and there. He kept driving until he was close to the west entrance. He pulled into a parking area and opened the trailer.

Sheik was ready. Langley threw both gym bags, held together by a sturdy rope, on Sheik's back, then settled into the saddle himself. It was after dark and no one was in the area. He rode Sheik to the little swamp that sat on the southern border of his grandparents' property. He considered the swamp briefly–he was less likely to be seen–but turned around and rode to Wolf Lake instead.

Wolf Lake had been his view every miserable morning when he looked out his bedroom window.

Langley saw the glow of a television inside the house his grandparents had once lived. He urged Sheik into a slower pace to reduce the volume of the sound his hooves made on the hard gravel. He led him onto the softer shoulder and there was virtually no sound at all. They stopped on the west bank, far enough from the house to avoid detection, Langley thought. He unzipped the first canvas bag and removed the plastic-covered torso. Carefully, he snipped a number of holes in the bottom.

He held his breath when hoisted the weight with both hands to shoulder level and threw it in the lake. "Plunk". Langley allowed himself a quick look at the house, then did the same with the second bag. "Plunk".

Wolf Lake it was.

Langley sighed. Why did he feel let down? Disappointed? Had the days of torture with his second concubine been too short? Had the end come too quickly?

He had followed the same plan, the same time frame he used for his first concubine. With Eve I he had never been higher, more uplifted, in his life–including all his hours on Sheik's back. There must be something he missed with Eve II he couldn't bring to mind. Langley thought it would get better each time.

He was convinced the next time it would be.

9.

Faced with rush hour traffic, Mandy Zubinski and I agreed to leave at seven-thirty Tuesday morning to get to the BCA by nine. At seven, I had the necessary paperwork completed for the evidence we were submitting. I ran into Smoke in the break room.

"Will coffee help?" I asked, stifling a yawn.

Smoke handed me the cup he had poured for himself. "I'm hopin'. You sleep last night?"

He made the best coffee–strong, almost espresso. I closed my eyes to fully appreciate the first sip before I answered.

"Not much. I actually preferred being awake to the bad dreams I had when I did conk out." I shuddered. "I would shake peoples' hands and the person would disappear, but their detached arm would still be moving. That went on for about half the night. The other half I was finding body parts–mostly heads–in random places. Remind me never to open the trunks in my bedroom or living room ever again."

Smoke smiled slightly and nodded. "I had horses in most of my dreams, and when they got close, I saw their riders were headless. My *Sleepy Hollow* DVD is going in the trash first chance I get."

"I hear ya."

Smoke leaned back against the counter, sucked in a small sip of coffee, and rested the cup on his chest. "By the way, I got a hold of Darin on his cell this morning. He'll escort you around the BCA."

I raised my eyebrows. "And I suppose he'll want an update on my love life."

"He was pretty smitten with you when he met you last month." Smoke studied me above the rim of his cup.

"So, if he asks, what are you going to tell him, about your love life?"

I had been dating a man named Nick Bradshaw for several weeks.

I added more coffee to my cup. "'It's none of your business?'" I shrugged. "I don't know—not much to tell. I see Nick when I can, which isn't all that often." I lowered my voice in case anyone was in ear shot. "Plus, I don't need Zubinski to have something else on me to gossip about."

Smoke spoke quietly in turn. "Like I've said before, I think she's just jealous because she doesn't seem to fit in around here."

"It doesn't help that she has a crush on you," I added.

Zubinski called my cell at seven-twenty. "Want me to drive?"

"Thanks, but I got the evidence in my trunk already."

"Okay, I'll meet you by your squad."

The Winnebago County courthouse complex sat in the center of Oak Lea, overlooking Bison Lake, one of four lakes in the city. The sun had risen about an hour before and its reflection cut a low, bright path across the water. The still morning did not allow a ripple on the smooth-as-glass surface. I was mesmerized by the beauty of it on the walk to my car.

Zubinski and I nodded at each other and climbed into the vehicle. We were on the road by 7:25.

She was the first to speak. "I'm glad you're driving. Between thinking about what happened to that poor girl and worrying my alarm wouldn't wake me, I don't think I slept two hours last night."

I nodded. "I just hope we get the answers we need—who the victim is, for starters. And all we need is one good print from the killer."

"How about DNA? Those bites on her body—you'd think there might be some DNA left."

"I don't know—with her being in the water, that

might be gone–but I guess there could be traces. Let's hope."

I merged onto I-494 and was flanked a second later by semi-trucks on either side. As I sped up to ease my claustrophobia, my personal cell phone startled me. "Corky here."

"It's Sara. I didn't expect you to answer. I was just going to leave a message." Next to Smoke, Sara was my best friend.

"Hey! What's up?"

"The whole courthouse is buzzing with news of a dismembered body found up by Lake Pearl State Park. A dog found a woman's leg? Why didn't you tell me?"

I imagined the busy phone lines and mass emails sent from department to department.

"Things were a little hush-hush yesterday. And I didn't want to call you last night–it's not a good bedtime story."

"That's true. Oh my gosh, it is so awful! So what are doing up so early?"

I eased into the left lane to pass the slower traffic on the right. "Mandy Zubinski and I are on our way to the BCA with some evidence."

Sara made a half laugh, half "huh" sound. "Mandy Zubinski, as in the one with the big nose and the big mouth who started the rumor about you and Smoke having an affair?"

Sara was not soft spoken, and from the way Mandy squirmed in her seat, I knew she heard Sara's words. Time to hang up.

"Sara, I'll talk to you later. We're in heavy traffic."

"Okay. Later, then."

Mandy shifted slightly to face me. "Corky, for the record, I'm not the one who started that rumor. I admit, I did pass it on, though," Mandy said.

I glanced at her face. "Let's forget about it."

"I just wanted you to know. When I heard it, it seemed like it was true. You're with Detective Dawes all the time and it's obvious how much you like each other."

"He's an old friend of the family. He was my training officer and we happen to have a lot of cases together," I explained.

Mandy's voice softened. "Yeah. But I can sure see why you–or any woman–would want him."

Mandy still had a crush on Smoke all right.

When we pulled in the parking lot at the Minnesota Bureau of Criminal Apprehension, Mandy's eyebrows went up. "Oh! I didn't expect the BCA to be so huge. I was at the old facility on University. I had training there when I worked for Ottertail County. This campus is immense!"

"For sure. Just think, the four laboratory divisions alone have twelve separate sections."

"I guess." She was lost in the details of the building.

Zubinski and I slid our Winnebago County Sheriff Deputy I.D.'s through the slot at the bottom of the bullet-proof glass at the B.C.A.'s front desk. A uniformed woman close to sixty studied our photos, then looked at us.

"Darin Henning is expecting you. I'll let him know you're here."

"Thank you." I smiled at the officer when she returned our I.D.'s.

"You can set your bags in the sallyport." The officer glanced at the sealed evidence we carried in two paper bags and determined they posed no threat to the security of the bureau. She buzzed us into the inner sanctum to await the arrival of our escort.

Darin was all smiles when he approached and shook my hand.

"Hey, Ms. Sergeant Corky! Who's your friend?"

Friend.

Zubinski stepped forward and offered her hand. "Amanda Zubinski. Mandy."

Darin was near forty, about six feet tall, nice-looking–what my mother would describe as "cute"–with short, thinning, light brown hair.

His blue eyes twinkled. "Well, if I'm not a lucky

dog. Two beautiful women. I mean, it's always good to see Elton, but, hey! And I'm still a little peeved at him for keeping his nickname, 'Smoke' a secret from me. Why should I care how he got the name?" He shrugged.

Mandy's eyes widened. "How *did* he get it?"

"Oh, come on now, you too?" Darin's voice took on a conspiratorial tone. "Seems when he was a teenager he started a fish house on fire when he was making out with a girl. She made a joke of it, telling everyone, 'Where there's smoke there's fire and "Smoke's" real name is Elton.' Isn't that how it went?" He looked at me.

"Something like that," I mumbled.

There I was, caught in the middle of gossiping about Smoke, with Mandy taking in every word.

Darin clapped his hands together. "Okay, so Elton says you got a fingerprint card for victim I.D., garbage bags to look for latents, and, ah, casts of horse hooves?" His eyebrows went up as he read the last note.

I nodded as he read. "The detective thought you might be able to come up with a breed on the horse. If–um–when–we find the guy, his horse's prints at the scene will help us in court."

We stopped at the Trace Laboratory where we signed over the hoof casts.

Darin led the way to the Fingerprint Laboratory. "Corky, Mandy, this is Brandon–he is a whiz." We acknowledged the introductions, smiling or nodding. "If he can't get a match in Minnesota, he'll run them through the Midwest Automated Fingerprint Identification Network, or MAFIN. It's a database covering three states. If that doesn't turn up anything, he'll check AFIS, the Automated Fingerprint Identification System. There are literally million of prints there."

"Wow," Mandy said.

I handed our victim's fingerprint card containing prints of each individual finger, prints of the fingers on the right hand together, and prints of the fingers of the left hand together, to the capable Brandon.

Mandy and I followed Darin to another area of the

lab and he lowered his voice. "We'll check in with Shelly. Brandon is a whiz, but Shelly is the *original* whiz kid. If there are prints, or any partials to be found, she will find them. Guaranteed."

Shelly looked up from a microscope and frowned in a friendly way. "Hey, Darin, so you got company?"

Darin pointed at each of us as he spoke. "Shell, Mandy Zubinski. And you remember Corky Aleckson? She was here with Elton Dawes last month."

Shelly's frown deepened. "Oh, sure. You look older and much more official in uniform." She glanced at my collar brass.

"Isn't that the point?" Darin crossed his arms and nodded.

"Nice to see you again, Shelly." I handed her the package containing the garbage bags.

"They were in the water holding dismembered body parts?" she asked.

"Yes."

"We'll use the Alternative Vacuum Metal Deposition, or VMD technique. It's the most sensitive technique for developing fingerprints on non-porous articles such as plastic bags. And in this case, the major advantage is that it can detect fingerprints on articles that have been in water."

"That is so cool." Mandy's face lit up and I caught Darin staring at her.

"They're coming up with alternative methods to VMD, since we use a thin layer of gold followed by zinc. Gold, especially, has gotten so expensive. But how can you put a price tag on finding a murderer?" She raised her eyebrows.

My thoughts exactly.

"We'll leave Shelly to work her magic and go check on Brandon."

We crossed the lab again and found Brandon tapping away at his keyboard. Darin patted him on the shoulder. "What have you got, buddy?"

"A match. Her name's Molly Renee Getz."

Brandon pulled the sheet of information from his printer tray and handed it to me. Darin and Mandy closed in on either side, looking over my shoulders.

"Pretty blonde. What a shame." Darin clicked his tongue against the back of his teeth.

"She look familiar to you?" Mandy asked me.

I tried to place her. "A little bit."

"It's because she could be your sister, Corky," Darin chimed in.

She did look somewhat like me—when I got up in the morning, before I combed my hair.

"Twenty-seven years old. Address is Minneapolis," I noted.

"My age. Her mug shot, huh?" Mandy observed.

"Booked for prostitution, one week ago."

She was safely in jail only one week before. We studied her photo and vital statistics. The recollection of her other body parts would be with me forever. Now I had a face to add to the memory.

We will do everything we can to find the monster who tortured and killed you, I silently vowed to Molly.

My cell phone rang and knocked me out of my musing. "Sergeant Aleckson."

"It's me." Smoke. "How are things going down there?"

"We got an I.D. Molly Getz, twenty-seven, from Minneapolis."

"She's got a record?"

"Prostitution."

He let out a loud breath. "Well that opens the pool of suspects up to the size of Lake Superior. Damn. Anything on the garbage bags yet, any prints?"

"Not yet."

"You don't have to wait for the results. I just got a call from Melberg. The autopsy is set for twelve-thirty at the medical examiner's office. I signed you and Zubinski up to witness it. You may want to get a little something on your stomachs before that," he suggested.

"All right. Are they still located across the street

from Hennepin County Medical Center?"

"Yup."

"Okay. How's court going?"

"Still waiting to testify. We're on a fifteen minute recess–" he paused, "–which is over about now. Good luck."

"You, too." I clapped my phone shut and looked at Mandy. "We're the lucky ones that get to observe her–" I nodded at Molly's photo, "–autopsy."

Mandy's eyebrows shot up, her eyes huge. "I've never–"

Darin put an arm around her shoulder. "Just keep reminding yourself it's the least fun you'll have all week." He looked over at me. "What time is it set for?"

"Twelve-thirty."

He looked at his watch. "Ten-thirty now. Eating something light will help settle your stomachs."

"Yeah, that what Smoke said."

He smiled. "Come to think of it, he's probably the one who taught me that in the first place."

Darin guided us to a bright, airy cafeteria. "This will count as my coffee break–which I never usually take, by the way. They have great chicken noodle soup and I personally love their vegetable wraps." He rubbed his stomach.

Mandy chose Darin's suggestions and I got soup and yogurt. We were about to eat when Darin got a call. He frowned and stood up with his coffee, looking from Mandy to me. "I'm going to have to leave. Good to see you–say 'hi' to Elton." He pulled a card out of his pocket and handed it to Mandy. "If you want, give me a call sometime. Any time." With a small salute, he took off.

Mandy leaned in a little. "He sure is nice. And pretty cute, too."

My mouth was full so I didn't have to answer.

"How does he know Detective Dawes so well?"

I chewed another second, then swallowed. "They worked together in Lake County. Darin was a deputy before he became the Forensic Science Supervisor in the

Criminalistics Laboratory here."

"I wonder why he left law enforcement?"

"Not sure." I looked at my watch. "We should head out."

"Yeah, I'd rather be early." We threw our paper and plastic in the trash and stacked the trays. "Have you ever been to an autopsy before?" Mandy asked.

I nodded. "Two, actually. One was a woman who allegedly shot herself holding the gun in her left hand—she was right-handed. Turns out, her right hand was broken, they figured from a fall. Kind of a weird deal. The other one was a drug overdose. The guy laid there at a party all night and no one checked on him. They all thought he was just passed out."

"Man." She shook her head. "I have to confess I'm a little freaked out about this."

"Me too," I agreed.

Dr. Melberg, Mandy, and I stood in the autopsy room, waiting for the inevitable. Dr. Peter Jarvis was checking out the tools. He was in his mid-fifties and extremely tidy looking. His scrubs appeared starched and pressed and I searched for an errant hair, but didn't find one on his head, his eyebrows, or in either ear. Dr. Choua Vang was close to forty and very intense. She was so petite, I felt gargantuan next to her. The attendant, Scott Stevens, was thin and gawky and gave the impression he was uncomfortable in his own skin.

The two pathologists set to work. Stevens took notes and photos, and Dr. Melberg, Mandy, and I served as witnesses.

First they conducted an external examination of the five body parts, beginning with the limbs.

"Ligature marks on her wrists and ankles, indicating she was bound. Very clean cuts. I would say he used a bone saw like butchers use," Dr. Jarvis began.

"He's a butcher, all right," Mandy muttered quietly near my ear.

"She was still in rigor when she was found. Doc—"

Dr. Jarvis' eyes narrowed on Melberg, "–you recorded her core temp of seventy-five degrees Fahrenheit at sixteen-thirty hours yesterday. The water where she was found was seventy-two degrees, close to what the air temperature was as well."

Melberg cleared his throat. "That's correct."

"So, she hadn't yet reached the environmental temp." Dr. Vang surmised, touching the skin on the torso. "No adipocere." She looked at Mandy and me and explained, "The subcutaneous adipose, or fatty tissue of corpses, when immersed in cold water–or kept in plastic bags–can undergo a fairly uniform formation of adipocere. The superficial layers of skin actually slip off. This happens more on heavier people and . . . children." She paused. "You can see her skin's intact, which supports what her temperature indicates. She was dead twenty-two or twenty-three hours. I estimate death between seventeen-thirty and eighteen-thirty Sunday."

Between five-thirty and six-thirty the previous evening.

Unfortunately, I had been at one death scene where an older woman had died in the bathtub and was not found for several days. Her skin was *not* intact, which made for a very long, messy, and careful removal.

"From the–" Dr. Vang measured, "–two inches of neck which is still attached, we see the evidence of strangulation. No ligature marks on her neck. Killer used his hands, not a rope or wire or other means."

Dr. Jarvis turned the torso on its side to examine the back. "Several bruises and what looks like one–two–three bite marks. Upper right arm, left breast, and upper right thigh." He looked at the pathologist taking the notes. "We'll swab each of those for DNA." The attendant dropped his notepad in his pocket and performed the tests then returned the torso to its back.

Jarvis examined further. "A fair amount of vaginal and rectal tearing and scarring." The female doc swabbed for semen.

"A point of interest: she worked as a prostitute,"

Melberg told him.

"So, that will make it difficult to positively sort out what the killer did and what others may have done. The tears do look fresh." Jarvis drew his brows together.

Dr. Vang picked up the scalpel and made the Y incision by cutting from each shoulder to mid-chest, then down to the pubic area, opening the victim. Mandy started coughing–the same response she had the previous day when we uncovered Molly's torso. By the time the doctor used the rib cutters and lifted out the breast bone, Mandy's pale face had a green tinge to it.

I put my hands on her waist and guided her to a chair. "Why don't you sit down?" The last we needed was for her to fall and split her head open. There was enough trauma in the room already.

The doctors weighed and examined each vital organ.

"No head to be found?" Vang asked me.

"No. We scoured the lake with divers and sonar. We even checked a nearby swamp," I said

"Well, if a dog found her leg, maybe some wild creature found her head and carried it off somewhere," the female doc offered.

"If I only had a brain," Jarvis said dryly.

Dr. Vang's lips tugged to the left in a wry smile.

Mandy and I managed to get caught in afternoon rush hour traffic, also. "You want to go through a drive-through? Get something to eat?" I asked.

Mandy's color was back, but her face was strained. "No, thanks. All I want to do is get back to my apartment, take a very long shower, and find the funniest thing I can to watch on TV."

Comedy was the polar opposite of the past two days' events. "Sounds like a good idea."

"And thanks for not giving me a hard time about feeling sick back there. I can just hear Weber when he finds out."

I looked over at her. "Weber pick on you?"

"Not really, he just thinks every stupid thing I do is funny."

"Mandy, he's not going to find out unless you tell him," I assured her.

She smiled. "Thanks."

"You know, there are a lot of guys in the department who like to give each other grief–take it with a grain of salt. There are things in my life my fellow deputies–as much as I trust and care about them–will never know." I raised my eyebrows and grinned. "I hope."

"I think sometimes I try too hard to fit in."

Smoke had nailed it on the head. "Just be yourself."

Mandy smiled and said, "thanks," once more.

10.

After dropping Mandy off at her vehicle, I drove home wondering what a warped monster–one who tortured a woman, cut her apart, and threw her dismembered parts into a lake–might look like. Young, middle-aged? Most likely not elderly. Was he handsome? Was he her boyfriend, another family member, or a stranger? Did he lure her by acting charming, or by appearing to need help: like a Jeffrey Dahmer or a Ted Bundy?

A warm shower eased some tension, but didn't relax me. Actually, I wasn't ready to relax. I needed to find out all I could on dismemberment cases. I sat at my computer and pored through search engines, researching and reading until my eyes blurred from exhaustion.

The cases were gruesome and chilling. As I had told Sara–very poor bedtime stories.

In Brazil, seven youngsters were shot and dismembered as a result of a fight between gangs to control drug trafficking in the area. A man in Texas killed his girlfriend, dismembered then burned her to cover his crime. A teen in Japan beheaded his mother. There were cases in Pennsylvania, Louisiana, El Salvador, Guatemala, Israel. An horrific violent offense that crossed economic, cultural, racial, and social lines. But why?

I phoned Nick first, then Sara, and answered every question I could about the case and how I was doing. It was too early for bed and I was too tired to read anything distracting and fun. I didn't feel like eating or watching television. It was one of the rare times I didn't know what to do with myself.

My mother called at seven-thirty.

"Hi, dear, just checking in. You still able to help me get ready for the party this weekend?"

"As far as I know, Mom." I filled her in on the

events from the past two days in case something happened that would require me to work on the weekend.

My mother gasped. "That is the worst thing I have ever heard! I'm surprised it's not all over town."

"We had a gag order yesterday. The sheriff lifted it this afternoon, after we were able to make an identification. It's pretty bad, all right."

"Oh! I'm getting a call from your brother. I better take it. I hope John Carl isn't cancelling out on this weekend."

My mother, the worrywart. "Say 'hi' for me." My brother and his wife lived in Colorado.

I had barely hung up when Smoke called.

"Up for the next round?"

A tightness gathered around my middle. "And that is?"

"I just finished talking with Glen Olansky, homicide sergeant with Minneapolis. Our victim had a roommate and she let the officers look through Getz's things—personal papers, letters, etc. Roommate said Getz moved up here from Kansas a few weeks ago. Her parents are still there. Kansas City has a uniform on the way over there to make notification."

I thought of Molly's family and wondered what kind of people they were.

"Bad deal. Anyhow, I set up a meeting with Olansky tomorrow at 0800. You should be there."

"Sure."

"I'll swing by and pick you up at six-thirty."

"Uniform or street clothes?"

"Street."

The Homicide Investigative Division of Minneapolis Police Department was housed in City Hall. We found Room 180 and Sergeant Glen Olansky. He was a bear of a man—six-foot four or five, two hundred-fifty pounds, prematurely gray at forty.

Olansky had a stocky Latino officer beside him. "Detective, Sergeant, this is Inspector Jesse Hernandez.

He commands the First Precinct where we believe Molly Getz was picked up."

Both Olansky and Hernandez stared at me long enough to make me feel I should check for egg on my face.

Hernandez nodded and broke the silence. "According to Getz's roommate, she worked Hennepin Avenue, usually around Seventh Street."

"What's the roommate's name?"

"Oh, um . . ." Olansky checked his report. "Polly Rose Kline."

Smoke raised an eyebrow. "Molly's roommate's name is Polly?"

Olansky smirked. "You think I make this stuff up? That's the name on her I.D."

"Molly and Polly, makes it easy to remember," I added.

"When was the last time Kline saw Getz?" Smoke asked.

Olansky referred to the report. "Thursday night about ten. Kline said Getz was on Hennepin, between Seventh and Eighth. Kline got home late—no Getz. Got up the next day—still no Getz. When it got toward evening, Kline called her cell, but there was no answer. Kline was starting to get concerned at that point."

Smoke furrowed his eyebrows. "Is there a pimp?"

"No. According to Kline, Getz was an independent."

"That could make a lotta pimps mad," Hernandez added.

"Could, sure."

"Any enemies? Boyfriend? Jealous johns?" I asked.

"None of the above." Olansky threw the report on the desk. "There is something else."

"What's that?" Smoke asked.

"Four weeks ago we had another streetwalker go missing. One Amber Ferman. Take a look at her mug shot." She had shoulder length blonde hair, and facial features similar to Molly Getz.

"They could be sisters," Smoke observed.

"Look at the height and weight on the rap sheets. Ferman: five-foot-four, one-hundred-twenty pounds. Getz: five-foot-five, one-hundred-fifteen pounds." Olansky walked over to where I was sitting. He held the two photos, one in each hand, on either side of my face.

"What's your height and weight, if you don't mind?"

"Five-five, one-hundred-ten."

"Not planning on any street-walking in Minneapolis, are you?"

"Not anymore," I quipped.

Olansky lowered his voice and kept his eyes trained on me. "We'd been studying those mugs and then you walked in and it was like I had a vision. We've been in the business long enough to know it doesn't take much to get people on the wrong path sometimes. Drugs, booze, gambling, you know."

Olansky's cell phone rang. He pulled it from its case on his belt, glanced at the face, hit a button, and laid it on his desk.

He continued, "I've gotten a little jaded in my twenty years here. But, like I started to say—Sergeant, when you walked in, I imagined for a second Molly Getz was standing there. It gave me new resolve to find the vile creature who cut her up. And also, to find Amber Ferman. My gut tells me the two cases are connected."

A tingling sensation ran through me. "Doesn't bode well for Ferman."

"No, it does not."

"Are you in a hurry to get home?" Smoke asked.

We were at a stoplight in Medina, a Minneapolis suburb.

"Not especially. Why?"

"Gil's office is about a mile from here. I thought we'd drop in and harass him a minute."

"Go for it."

Gilbert Dawes was Smoke's younger brother. He was an engineer with the Hennepin County Transportation Department.

Smoke looked at his watch. "He should be there, I'm guessing. Haven't seen much of him or his family this sumer. His boys play baseball and when they get a free weekend, they head to their cabin."

I turned toward Smoke. "You've been to a few of their games, haven't you?"

"Oh, yeah. But, as you know, it's been a busy at work. Doesn't seem to let up."

"That is the truth."

I'd met Smoke's brothers a couple of years before. Smoke invited their families over for a barbeque and discovered he was out of gas when he tried to fire up his grill. He called to see if I had a tank. I did. I disconnected it from my grill and took it over. Smoke asked me to stay for dinner, but I didn't.

Gil and his wife Lora had three teenagers, two boys and a girl. Smoke's older brother, Charles–Chaz–and his wife Cindy had three girls and one boy. Two were in college and two were in high school.

"What brings my big brother and the lovely Ms. Aleckson to my door?"

Gil rose from his chair and came around to our side of the desk when we stepped into his office. He shook my hand first, then turned to Smoke. They locked their right hands and threw their left arms around the other's shoulders. A hand shaking hug.

Gil had dark brown hair that curled up at his collar. His eyes were a paler shade of blue than Smoke's. Family photos were lined on a shelf behind his desk. I studied them while Smoke explained.

"We're on our way back from Minneapolis, so as long as we were in the neighborhood–"

"Glad you stopped. A bad deal you got going on in Winnebago, huh?"

Gil waved his hand at two office chairs as he sat on a third. Smoke and I took our seats.

"Yes, it is." Smoke sumarized the case.

"El, what have you got planned for Labor Day, again?"

"I'm the investigator on call Friday and Saturday, and Kristen's party is Sunday."

"Oh, that's right. I forgot you were on call." Gil looked at me. "When I was a sophomore in high school, I had the biggest crush on your mom, who was a senior, of course."

"A lotta guys had a crush on Kristen."

Gil nodded. "Including you, El."

Smoked shrugged.

"You're a pretty good mix of both your parents in looks—you got the best of both," Gil told me.

"Thanks."

He turned his attention back to Smoke. "We're heading up to the cabin for the one last hurrah of the sumer. Too bad you can't join us. Chaz called a while ago. His whole crew can make it this year."

Smoke nodded. "Occupational hazard. Are you going to keep the cabin open through hunting season again this year?"

"Oh, yeah. We won't winterize it until after deer season."

"Good." Smoke slapped his thigh. "Well, we best get back on the road and let you get back to work."

"Thanks for stopping. We haven't seen enough of each other lately, El. And good to see you again, Corky." Gil smiled.

I smiled back. "You, too."

"Have a safe trip home and say 'hi' to your mother."

"Will do," Smoke and I said together.

11.

Langley watched the DVDs of the last days in the lives of his concubines, skipping ahead to the best parts. He had planned to wait another month to take his next concubine, then realized he should locate her and move in when the moment was right. It might take a while to find Eve III, after all. It was probably best to start looking sooner than later.

His phone rang and he jumped at the unexpected interruption, annoyed because it pulled him out of his excitement. His mother was the only one who ever called him and that was rare. He checked caller I.D. It was his mother, all right, but Langley couldn't answer. He needed time between the pleasure his concubines brought him and talking to the woman who burdened him with one nagging issue or the other.

He waited for the message–it might be about Sheik. Langley would want to know about that right away. No, it was nothing. His parents had returned home after their latest jaunt. He should call when he had time.

Should and would were two different things entirely.

12.

Winnebago County Chief Deputy Mike Kenner was well trained to facilitate debriefing sessions. He was an effective leader, sought after by area police departments, fire departments, ambulance services, and neighboring counties, following any number of critical incidents: car crashes, house fires with burn victims, suicides, use of deadly force.

Kenner had served with the department for twenty years. He was close to six feet with broad shoulders, a longer torso, and shorter arms and legs. He enjoyed waterskiing and had developed a deep tan over the sumer. His brown hair was shaved on the sides and short on top in a typical military cut. I'd seen his brown eyes soften in kindness or harden in anger, depending on the circumstances. They were neutral, almost guarded, that day.

"Welcome everyone. I'm glad to see so many of you here after Monday's discovery and recovery efforts. Anyone here *not* been part of a debriefing before?" He lifted his right hand like he was taking an oath.

Ortiz and Holman, both recent hires, raised their hands.

"Good. The purpose is to help you understand what happened, and to help you understand that you had no *control* over what happened. In this case, to victim Molly Getz. You need to take the incident out of your short term memory and put it in your long term memory. Make sense?"

It made sense to me, and I needed help to make it a reality.

Kenner looked from face to face. "You are not in this alone. We're going to work through it together. Okay, how many of you have had trouble getting the images of dismembered body parts out of your heads?"

Everyone in the room raised his or her hand.

Kenner nodded. "After a traumatic event, our minds keep running what happened, over and over. We need to stop that process for our own peace of mind. Anyone here wonder why and how someone would torture, kill, and dismember another human being?"

Again, every hand went up. Kenner pulled a dry erase marker from his breast pocket.

"Okay. First, I want each of you to describe your experience at Wolf Lake, and your part in the investigation we've been conducting the past two days. What I'm looking for here are the facts."

We each shared our roles in the events. Mason, Carlson, and Weber described feeling around the murky water for the body parts and bringing them to shore. Zubinski shared her questioning Mr. Engen, assisting with the body parts after they were removed, and the autopsy experience.

Smoke was the first on the scene and had the initial contact with Mrs. Engen and the leg. In addition to everything that happened at Wolf Lake, he also relayed the details of the visit to the Minneapolis Police Department. Some of the deputies had little direct involvement, but told what they had done. The sheriff gave his version.

I echoed what Smoke, Zubinski, and the others reported.

The chief deputy assured us that our reactions and emotions were appropriate and very normal. "From what you have all reported, the most prominent common thought is that having the dismembered body of a young woman, in one of our local lakes, is something none of you had ever thought of as a possible crime scenario. You are horrified by it."

We glanced around at each other, checking reactions. Some nodded, a few agreed out loud. Mandy caught my attention for a shared moment then my eyes met and held Smoke's for another.

The chief deputy's voice drew me back to his face.

"Okay, now tell me: what was the worst thing for you, personally? You had different roles in the discovery and recovery. What got you the most?"

For Smoke, it was being first on the scene, mentally processing that he was actually looking at a dismembered leg while he attempted to calm the PR–person reporting. Mason said it was finding the arm on the lake bottom and having to hold it. The other divers said discovering the garbage bags and feeling the body parts in them was the worst. Some said the shock of the leg lying on the grass hit them the hardest. Mandy said it was seeing the torso with the evidence of violence on it.

As awful as the discovery had been, the worst thing for me was learning the victim's identity and wondering who had brutalized her in such a way, and why he had done it.

After acknowledging each of our worst moments with care and concern, Kenner pressed on. "So tell me, what symptoms are you having? Any trouble sleeping? Nightmares, nervousness, what?"

Weber cleared his throat. "I dreamed I was on patrol, saw a guy throw bags in the water. When he turned toward me, he had one of those scary-guy masks. And–I'll fess up–I woke up with my heart pounding pretty good."

I thought of Smoke's dream, then my own.

"I worry that when I get a call on the radio it'll be the discovery of another dismembered body," Mandy admitted.

I hadn't thought of that.

"I'm thinking when I'm fishing, I'll reel in an arm or a leg," Carlson said.

I hadn't thought of that, either. Swimming and water sports, common to most of us, presented a potential new threat.

Everyone admitted to trouble sleeping.

Kenner rubbed his hands together and lowered his voice to a soothing, almost hypnotizing level. "Each one of you is expressing completely normal, expected reactions. You have each other, you have me, you have other members of the department. Talk about your feelings. I know that isn't always easy, especially in our profession, but it is important. Talk to your friends, family, loved ones."

His voice gained volume with the next instructions. "Eating well is important. Exercise is important. Don't abuse alcohol. If you're having problems, come talk to me or one of your colleagues, or see a doctor. You are all valued members of the Winnebago Sheriff's Department and we want you, we need you, to stay healthy. Untreated symptoms often lead to Post Traumatic Stress Syndrome and we all want to avoid that. Any questions?"

Our session lasted two hours and I was on information overload. When no one responded, Kenner smiled and clapped his hands together. "Okay then. I'll turn this over to Detective Dawes for some updates."

Smoke grabbed the file from the table, stood, and faced the group. "We got some info back from the BCA on the photos, and measurements of the suspect vehicle and horse trailer tires we sent 'em. The tires are Ford factory. From the measurements of the front and rear tracks, they were able to identify the vehicle as an Expedition."

"Just need a year and color, huh?" Mason voiced.

Every deputy jotted the information on memo pads.

Smoke slid his readers onto his nose and glanced at the report. "By taking the distance of the horse trailer wheels to the SUV, and the distance between the tires, they identified the trailer as being ten feet long and six feet wide. The tires are two-hundred-twenty-five by fifteen-inch Goodyear, which are standard on a trailer made by a company called A-1 Trailers. I got a picture of what it looks like."

Smoke handed the picture to me. The trailer was white with silver trim and a round front. It had a full front door in the nose, in addition to the back doors: a unique model. I passed the photo on.

"If you spot an Expedition pulling that trailer, do

not stop it without backup. It will be a probable cause felony stop."

Smoke gave a rundown of our meeting with Sergeant Olansky and Inspector Hernandez from the Minneapolis Police Department, and passed Molly Getz's photo around the room. Every deputy studied it carefully and quietly.

Carlson leaned over and said, "Corky, notice she looks kinda like you?"

I nodded. "Me and about ten percent of every other woman my age in Minnesota."

"Not all blue-eyed blondes are quite as cute as you."

There was nothing to do but roll my eyes.

13.

For the past ten years, my mother had held an end-of-sumer shindig on Labor Day weekend. She had the perfect spot for the party–a huge barn so old the wood was practically petrified. It had been some time since animals actually lived there. When it belonged to my grandfather and his father before that, dairy cows, cattle, and a few horses spent nights there when they came in from the pastures. Pigs, sheep, chickens, and turkeys had other accommodations on the farm.

I found my mother in the barn, sweeping down a cobweb, the day before the party. "Hey, Mom, I'm here to help."

"Corinne! I didn't hear you coming–you startled me." She leaned against her broom and fingered away some hair that had fallen across her face. "Well, what do you think?"

I began my perusal by starting with my favorite view: straight up. The center and main part of the barn was a hexagon that rose twenty-four feet to the roof. The six sides tapered and met in the apex. From the outside, the cupola–a miniature model of the barn sitting on the peak–was visible. A copper weathervane of cut and hammered letters N, S, E, and W were attached to dowels, pointing the four directions. A Belgian workhorse, supported by a pole, stood on top.

The hay lofts were positioned as balconies about halfway between the floor and roof, on all six sides. There were openings on each of the walls, covered by wooden doors. My mother had glass installed in the openings and kept the doors open to let the sunlight in. When I was a child, I loved climbing the steps to the lofts. I would lie on my back on a blanket of hay and watch the clouds pass by the windows, picking out shapes and figures as they moved and changed.

My mother had cleared the lofts of hay some time before, and had half-walls and railings installed. She accumulated a variety of garage sale tables and chairs and painted them fun colors. People at her parties enjoyed sitting on the loft areas to relax, visit, eat, and watch the dancing below. There were a few couches on the inside walls. On occasion, I would retreat on one to watch the clouds pass by and daydream again.

In addition to the hexagon main section, two wings jutted out from the back sides. They had housed the dairy cows and cattle. Horses were kept in the center part, but Mother had the stanchions removed when she decided to turn the structure into a dance barn. The ground floor consisted of wide ironwood planks and served as a fine, though not necessarily perfect, dance floor. Large glass picture windows, dressed with gingham curtains, were on the three available sides of the hexagon.

My great-grandfather, assisted by his brother, had designed and constructed the barn. Neighbors helped raise it with sturdy ropes and strong bodies. The barn, built to last, had withstood over one hundred years of Minnesota climate extremes: from sixty degrees below zero to over one hundred degrees above, as well as rain, hail, gusting straight line winds, freezing drizzle, blizzards. My great-grandfather made the weathervane with his simple tools.

"Gosh, Mom, what did you do? Scrub the floors, for heaven sakes?"

The barn had stopped smelling like animals long before.

"I don't know why you always give me a hard time about that. A mop with a little Murphy's Oil Soap does make a big difference." She grinned, bringing her laugh lines to life.

My mother was almost fifty, but retained a youthful look despite the time she devoted to worrying about everything possible. She was widowed with two children when she was in her early twenties–a good explanation for why she worried as she did. Mother was slightly curvy and naturally thin. We shared gray eyes and blonde hair–hers was wavy, mine was straight. I had two inches of height on her.

Long tables, covered with cloths, stood against the two side walls to the immediate right and left of the front double doors. One would hold a smorgasbord of food and the other a variety of beverages. Wash tubs on the floor would be filled with ice for soft drinks, bottled water, and beer.

The wall opposite the front door provided the backdrop for where the band played. Strings of white lights hung on the loft railings and around the outer wall on the main floor. More colorful garage sale tables and chairs were arranged under the loft area and helped to brighten the space.

"Okay, so what's left to do? Everything looks done." I took another look around.

"We'll need extension cords from the storage room for the band and the food tables. And if you want, you can do a last weeding in the flower beds. I have the food pretty well under control."

Extension cords and weeds I could handle.

"What time is John Carl getting in?" I asked.

"His plane arrives at three, so by the time he picks up his car, he figures he'll be here around five," Mother explained.

I looked down at the clean wood planks, then at my mother. I weighed my words. "Mom, I have to tell you something that has been bothering me for a while."

She leaned on her broom. "What is it, dear?"

"You know that night you had Smoke over for dinner?"

"Of course." Her words held a hesitancy.

I didn't want to embarrass my mom, but I had to clear the air. "Well, I stopped by to drop off your salad bowl and I saw you and Smoke making out, pretty hot and heavy, in your kitchen."

My mother's complexion darkened until her rose

colored shirt became the perfect camouflage for her neck and face. She turned the exact shade in seconds.

"Corinne Mae Aleckson!" She set her broom aside and propped her hands on her hips. "Not that it's really any of your business, but since you brought it up, I'll tell you exactly what happened."

"Okay." *But remember, I'm your daughter so spare me any intimate details.*

"You know Elton and I have been friends since junior high, and he was your father's best friend." She paused for a brief smile. "After me, that is. Anyway, Elton and I have always liked each other. He, especially, thought there might be more to it. We tried a little experiment, you know, to see just what might be there. And, as it turns out, the spark was missing–for both of us."

"From what I saw, you were in the middle of a pretty passionate kissing session," I argued.

Her color was returning to normal. "What you saw was us *trying* to make it passionate. It just didn't work. We gave up after a couple of minutes, started laughing, and picked up where we left off, with our friendship the way it was."

"Sorry, Mom."

"Sorry for what?"

I gave her a brief hug. "That Dad had to die so young, that you haven't found someone else."

She looked down for a bit. "It's funny. I knew your father my entire life, and when he left for Vietnam, I never thought he *wouldn't* come back. I thought we would be together for another sixty or so years. When I dream about him, he is still this handsome young twenty-year-old. Then I wake up and look in the mirror and think, 'what would Carl want with an old woman like me for?'"

I put a hand on each of her shoulders and gave her a slight shake. "Okay, reality check here. Mother, I know you are closing in on fifty, but a *lot* of people ask if you're my older sister. And I seriously don't understand why you are not all wrinkles the way you fret about everything."

"I don't," she defended herself.

"You have it down to a science."

A Dodge Intrepid pulled into Mother's driveway right after I finished my chores. John Carl got out, a broad smile on his normally serious face. I ran to him and we held each other tightly. He was only ten months old when I was born and we were close, despite being direct opposites and living eight hundred miles apart. But, as different as we were, we shared the same core beliefs and principles. Mother tapped his shoulder and he grabbed her into a warm embrace. By the time they separated, Mom had tears streaming down her cheeks.

"John Carl, you are so skinny!" I noticed.

"Not exactly skinny," he protested.

Mother pulled the neck of her shirt up to dab at her wet cheeks. "Dear, have you been sick?"

"No, I just forget to eat sometimes," he admitted.

A concept I couldn't relate to. "Have no fear, John Carl, Mother will not let you forget such a thing while you're here." I decided to enter a touchy area. "You said Emily couldn't make it–what's up?" Emily was the sister-in-law I had seen a mere three times in five years, including their wedding.

"She couldn't get the weekend off work. No one would trade with her."

"Didn't she put in for days off months ago? This is an annual event," I countered.

"Just drop it, Corky." *Okay.* I tried to make eye contact with my brother in an attempt to figure out what he wasn't telling us, but John Carl turned to his rental car, popped open the trunk, and pulled out his suitcase.

It had been months since the three of us–Mother, John Carl and I–had sat down for dinner together. Mom made our favorite meal: spaghetti, garlic bread, and a romaine lettuce salad tossed with marinated artichoke hearts and black olives, and topped with Caesar dressing.

Mother set her fork down and leaned closer to my brother. "John Carl, tell us how everything is going. You never talk about yourself."

John Carl swirled his bread around in the spaghetti sauce on his plate then leaned back in his chair. He glanced at his food before looking at Mom. "Emily and I are having some problems."

"What kind of problems?" she asked.

He crossed his arms on his chest. "She's been staying away from home more and more. She says I work too much."

"We all know you put in a lot of hours at work then you go home and work some more," I said.

John Carl's shoulders raised in a shrug. "I won't argue with that. I like to work." His fingers began tapping on his elbows. "But, there's more to it than that. You know her schedule. She works every other weekend and has days off during the week. I work during the week. Emily's doing stuff with her friends more and more all the time. She'd rather be with her friends than with me." His arms dropped to the table.

"How can you say that?" My mother always tried to give others the benefit of the doubt.

"She told me. Actually, she said she has more fun with her friends than she has with me."

The stunned look on Mother's face must have been a mirror to my own. Mother reached over, laying her hand on his. "Have you talked to your pastor, or a marriage counselor?"

John Carl flicked a glance my way. He confessed to me he had seen a psychologist a while back, but hadn't mentioned any marital problems, or seeing anyone recently.

"I did talk to a shrink, but Emily wouldn't go with me. She said I'm the one with the problems, not her."

I lost a lot of respect for my sister-in-law in that one sentence.

He frowned. "Can we talk about something else?"

"Nice weather we're having," I joked.

John Carl's forehead furrowed deeper and he looked at me the same way my mother did nearly every day of my life—with care and concern. "Corky, are you all healed up after your near-death experience last month? I don't see any battle scars."

None that showed.

I swallowed my food. "Um, honestly? I'm still working through a few things." My mother's surprised expression made me pause. "And now I have something else to deal with—Alvie Eisner wants to see me, about something personal, no less."

"That awful woman tried to kill you!" Mother blurted out.

"Yes, Mother. And I wish people would quit reminding me of that. I was there. Trust me, I remember every detail of that night."

My brother leaned forward. "Did you tell her to kiss off, that you wouldn't see her?"

"John Carl!"

John Carl and I shared a smile at our mother's reprimand.

"I said I'd see her after her trial, which, by the way, starts week after next." I licked my fork and laid in on my plate.

Mother's voice grew soft. "I just keep thinking of that poor little granddaughter of hers. She's in my prayers every night. I hope she can find a good home, good people to love her."

Ten-year-old Rebecca Eisner: daughter of a felon, granddaughter of a murderer.

I nodded. "Rebecca's future weighs on my heart, too. I've been advised not to see her until after the trial, but at least I hear she's doing pretty well with her foster family."

We thought in silence for a while.

John Carl grabbed another piece of bread. "Tell me more about the famous case you got going on now."

Infamous case was a better description.

"Nothing much to add to what I wrote in the

emails. Except, we did have a debriefing yesterday."

"That help?" John Carl asked between chews.

"Yes, it really does. The chief deputy is a very good facilitator."

Mother's eyes moved from John Carl to me and back again.

"You have a debriefing after the Eisner incident?" he wondered.

"Not exactly. Sara and I met with a psychologist. I was supposed to go back, but my schedule has been kinda crazy."

He shook his bread at me. "Face your demon."

Which one? There were so many demons in my line of work.

14.

When the sheriff reached his saturation point with media requests, he handed them over to Smoke as the lead investigator. It was the top regional news story for three consecutive nights. We expanded our investigation to encompass a broader base of area residents to query and question. People called in with leads, reporting sightings of lone riders on horses in Lake Pearl State Park and around the area. The riders' descriptions ranged from teenage boys to middle-aged women to older men.

None of the reported riders were seen toting bags large enough to hold body parts. No surprises there. If I had killed and dismembered another human being, I would take great pains to avoid getting caught with the evidence of my demented crime.

After an exhausting week of dealing with all the aspects of such a horrendous crime, everyone in the sheriff's department was weary. I looked forward to an evening of socializing and semi-relaxation at my mother's party.

Her excited tone brought me out of my reverie. "John Carl, Corinne! Will you carry the rest of the food out?"

Mother had cooked and baked for days, apparently for an army. We set cold dishes in bowls of ice and hot dishes on warmers. Mother's barn began to fill with people at five that evening, carrying in potluck dishes to add to the food-laden tables. It was an impressive feast. The five piece old-time band was ready to entertain us with waltzes, polkas, and country tunes until nine that night.

"You kids can help me keep track of guests when they arrive, in case I miss someone. Tell them to help themselves to food and drinks."

John Carl's face dropped slightly and he looked

like he was being sent into battle. He was not the make-small-talk-social-butterfly kind of guy.

"Will do, Mom," I promised.

Sheriff Twardy walked through the door and glanced around. He was wearing jeans and a plaid shirt and carrying a bottle of wine. I tried to recall a time I had seen him out of uniform and couldn't.

"Mother, what is the sheriff doing here?" I whispered.

"I invited him. It's been a bad week—he needs to have a little fun, too." Mother patted my arm and smiled.

"Why didn't you tell me my boss was coming?"

"Didn't I mention it, dear?" She left to greet the sheriff.

I looked at John Carl. "Okay, that is odd. Our mother has some major explaining to do."

John Carl shook his head in dismissal. "Corky, you're always so suspicious of everything."

"Mother could have warned me. Look at that!" I nudged John Carl when Mom gave the sheriff a small hug. "You don't think that's odd? Our mother hugging the Winnebago County Sheriff? I didn't know she knew him *that* well."

He shrugged. "Apparently she does."

Smoke showed up right behind the sheriff, shook his hand, and gave my mother a one arm hug. I walked over to greet both men. The sheriff's smile was easy and genuine and caught me slightly off guard. Mother passed the bottle of wine from the sheriff to me, and I held out my free hand to take Smoke's plate of venison sumer sausage slices.

"I got it, thanks. Just show me where you want it." He followed me to the food table.

"Smoke, did you know the sheriff was coming?"

"Yeah, he mentioned it."

I slid a platter over to make room for Smoke's dish. "Why didn't you tell me?"

"This being your mother's party, I thought you knew." He plopped down the plate.

"She expects to know every detail of my life, but she keeps her own pretty private."

His eyebrows moved together. "Yeah, I noticed she likes to talk about just about anything except herself. Always seemed like self-protection to me."

"What do you mean?"

"You can't get hurt if you don't let anyone in."

"Oh." John Carl was the same way.

Maybe I was too. A little.

I was still talking to Smoke when Nick Bradshaw, the man I was dating, arrived with his daughter and two of her friends. I waved them over.

"Sergeant Corky, hi! Thanks for inviting us. Dad, can we go play?" Faith said, her friends in tow.

Mother had games: bean bag toss, horse shoes, volleyball, and badminton set up on the lawn for both kids and adults.

"That's fine, but don't wander off." He smiled at the girls.

"Okay Dad, thanks." And off they ran.

"Corky, you look terrific, as always." Nick turned to me, slid an arm around my waist, and pecked my lips with his.

"What did you do to your hair?" He ran his fingers over some strands.

"Um, brushed it."

Smoke chuckled. I flushed.

"I mean, you know, I usually pull it back in a ponytail or a bun. I just brushed it down tonight." Why did I need to explain?

"Very becoming." He bent to whisper in my ear, "Very sexy. You are so incredibly gorgeous."

"Thanks, same to you," I said out loud, uncomfortable whispering in front of Smoke.

Nick's muscled physique worked well in a suit, shorts, or the jeans and light denim shirt he was wearing that night.

"Nick, I'd like you to meet Detective Elton Dawes, Smoke." I turned to Smoke and caught him studying Nick the same way he eyed suspects.

"Good to finally meet you, Detective. Corky sings your praises." Nick offered his hand, which Smoke accepted and shook.

"Really? So, I must be doing something right." Smoke's voice was flat.

Nick glanced at me, then back to Smoke. "Apparently. I understand you were her mentor in the department."

Smoke focused on me when he answered. "Corinne was a little wet behind the ears when she came on board, but what with her being a fast learner and good judge of character–" he paused and stared at Nick, "–she was one of my easier trainees."

Oh for heaven's sake!

Nick shifted, adjusted his belt buckle then reached around my shoulder and patted the top of my arm.

"Shall we dance?"

"You know how to polka?"

"I'm a fast learner, too." Nick grabbed my hand. "Excuse us," he told Smoke as he pulled me onto the dance floor.

"Why are you acting so nervous?" I asked, as if I didn't know.

Nick slipped his right hand on my waist and his left hand onto mine as we began to one-two-three around the room.

"Your Smoke made me feel like he was about to haul me off to an interrogation room."

"What?" I looked in his eyes.

"To find a reason you shouldn't be dating me."

"Smoke's in the habit of looking out for me. He was my father's friend and we've been through a lot together in my seven years with the department."

"I can understand that, but look at the way he is staring at us. He is more than looking out for you," Nick said.

I casually glanced around, spotting Smoke

seconds later. He attempted a little grin, enough to show his dimples, but the smile didn't reach his eyes.

"Well, we've got this big case going, as you know. He's been very preoccupied with that."

When John Carl sided over to Smoke, he finally looked away from us.

"So you've done some polkaing before," I said to change the subject.

"My mother's heritage is German and that's what we did at my cousins' wedding dances–polkas and waltzes. Lots of polka bands where I come from. We even have Polka Mass at church a few times a year," Nick explained.

"What exactly is a polka mass?"

"Instead of traditional hymns, you sing polka music hymns. It's actually a lot of fun–I'll take you sometime. There are quite a few in Carver County. I took Faith to two of them this sumer." Carver was the county south of Winnebago.

"I'd like that."

Nick guided me to the outer edge of the dancers when the next song, "Leichtensteiner Polka" began. He moved beside me and took my left hand in his. I reached my right hand up to grasp his right hand at shoulder level.

"You know the Domino? Right cross, right kick, step, step, step?" Nick asked.

"Sure do."

Once we began, other couples joined us and we danced in a circular motion around the room.

"*Ja, das ist die Liechtensteiner Polka, mein schatz, polka, mein schatz–*" Nick's baritone voice sang out until I spoiled the moment by laughing.

"Don't stop. You have a wonderful, deep voice."

"You weren't laughing *at* me, you were laughing *with* me?" He grinned.

"Neither! It just surprised me to hear you sing. In German, no less."

"I have my high school German teacher to thank for almost every German beer-drinking song I know."

I laughed again, trying to imagine Nick sitting in a classroom singing German songs.

"Which reminds me, I am suddenly very thirsty. Need a drink?" he asked.

"Thanks, you go ahead. I better mingle for a little bit."

I gazed up at the barn loft area. A few of my friends–Sara, Brian Carlson, Todd Mason, and his wife Kayla, were sitting at a table, eating and talking. Sara waved. I lifted my head in acknowledgement and smiled back. There were couples–some holding children–dancing between the tables, and oblivious to the people eating around them.

The main floor was more crowded. People tended to stay near the food, beverages, and band. I said my hellos as I walked by the guests. Some hovered close to the food tables, others sipped drinks while they conversed, laughed, and relaxed. Mother would be pleased with the turnout and the good time her guests were having. John Carl had not ventured from Smoke's side.

"Lose your partner?" Smoke asked when I joined them.

I spotted Nick talking to a small group by the drink table. "Temporarily, I guess. You two having any fun?"

"This isn't quite my scene," my brother complained.

I threw an arm around his shoulder and gave it a mild shake. "John Carl, for Mother's sake, try to find some enjoyment here. Pretend you are not such a serious workaholic for one night."

"Ouch," Smoke said.

"I'm sorry. John Carl, let me put it this way–kick back a little, talk to people, dance."

The worried, serious expression he wore so well appeared in force. "Corky, I hardly know most of these people. And who am I supposed to dance with?"

Right on cue, Sara stepped in beside me and gave me a half hug. Her jade green eyes were luminous and her strawberry blonde hair hung in soft waves halfway to her elbows.

"I am so glad I didn't go home this weekend! Why fight Labor Day weekend traffic when I can have such a great time here?" Sara turned to the men. "Hi, Detective. And you are John Carl, I presume?" Sara asked my brother, extending her hand.

He clasped her hand and nodded. "Just John to everyone outside my family."

"John Carl!" I sounded like my mother.

He held up his hands in protest. "I didn't mean it like that. I just meant my family are the only ones who call me John Carl."

"Because of your father, Carl, I guess?" Sara surmised and smiled. "I'm Sara Speiss. I can't believe we've never met before."

"Oh, my gosh! I should have introduced you earlier," I apologized. "When John Carl comes home for a visit, you always seem to be in Brainerd."

"I guess that's true."

"It's nice to finally meet you. Corky talks about you all the time." John Carl actually smiled.

"She talks about you all the time." Sara reached over and pushed his arm.

"John Carl was just saying he didn't have anyone to dance with. Sara, you don't mind having your feet tromped on by a big guy, do you?"

"Very funny." John Carl smiled. Again.

"I'd love to."

I leaned closer to Smoke. "I can't believe it. I don't remember the last time I saw John Carl dance–probably at his wedding."

"John Carl looks just like your father–both six feet tall, about one-eighty, broad shoulders, trim. But way more serious than Carl."

"Really?" I asked, watching them dance. "You know, if John Carl wasn't married, I'd say he and Sara would make a cute couple."

"Sara is very pretty, and likable too, as long as you

don't cross her, that is. I've seen her get downright angry at some of her probationers in court. She's almost had *me* trembling with fear when those green eyes of hers go three shades darker because some guy has broken his probation."

I laughed. "Yeah, right."

"I was dancin' with my darlin' to the Tennessee Waltz, when an old friend I happened to see–" the band singer began.

"Hey, they're playing our song," Smoke noticed. Years before, he had taught me to waltz at the first of my mother's parties he attended.

"For old-times' sake?" I offered my hand.

His grip was firm and when he captured me in his arms, he held me too closely and too securely for a casual dance. I inhaled his clean, woodsy scent and flashed back to the last time I was in his arms–the night I thought I was going to die. Smoke held me for a long time that night, and thereafter, whenever I awoke with night terrors of being suffocated by Alvie Eisner, I would remember Smoke's solid arms around me and the way he smelled. It would relax me, lull me back to sleep.

I pushed my memories aside. "You want to tell me what's been bothering you?" I asked.

"Don't you think he's a little too perfect?" He was obviously talking about Nick.

I pulled my head back enough to glimpse his face. "*Too* perfect? Is there such a thing?" I challenged.

"Handsome, good physique, prestigious career, affable–look at him over there, impressing the group around him." Old and young, men and women–my mother and the sheriff, included–appeared rapt, listening to a story I couldn't hear.

Smoke went on, "And he dances *and* sings."

"Smoke, you could have just described yourself and I don't think you're too perfect. At all." I held a deadpan face until he processed my words and a smile cracked his solemn expression.

"Sometimes, little lady–" Smoke brought our

extended arms closer to our bodies and turned my hand so our arms were intertwined. His hand on my back pressed my body still closer against him. The audible intake of my breath brought his focus back to my face. We searched each other's eyes, wondering what we were looking for, what would happen next.

An image of Smoke's near naked body sprang up from the recesses of my brain. I had accidentally seen him in his boxers one morning and was alarmed I found him so attractive, so desirable. My friend, my colleague. My lover? I kept my fascination repressed, but at that moment, locked against his body, I found myself feeling, not thinking.

"--Yes, I lost my little darlin' the night they were playing the beautiful Tennessee Waltz."

"I guess our song is over, Corinne," Smoke realized, his voice a mere whisper. We stopped dancing, but held our embrace to recover for another second.

"Right! Thank you." Formal, stilted, the best I could do.

"You've improved . . . every year." He took a step back, releasing one hand. The other, he slowly and gently lifted to his lips, and kissed my fingers. "Thank you."

My face betrayed me by blushing.

"Wow! You two are really good." Sara's voice brought me back to the party I had forgotten. Her happy expression was the exact opposite of John Carl's scowling one. Either Sara had offended him—which I doubted—or he did not approve of my dance with Smoke—which I did not doubt.

"Thanks!" I said too brightly. "Thanks, Smoke. Time to mingle."

Sara followed and pulled me aside. "Oh . . . my . . . God! That was so hot! I mean when you told me you were attracted to Smoke, I have to admit I thought you were a little nuts, but I see what you mean. He is a total hottie! Not that Nick isn't. No wonder you have such a dilemma."

"Sara, I don't want to talk about this here. And no, there can be no dilemma. I work with Smoke and I'm dating Nick." I looked her full in the face, took her hands in mine, and squeezed.

"Whatever." She pushed me away.

I was suddenly aware that Nick, Mother, the sheriff, my friends in the department, and others, may have witnessed the dance and wondered if something was going on between Smoke and me. Sara had. John Carl had.

I spotted my mother and the sheriff. They were sitting with my friends at a loft table and appeared lost in conversation. None of them were looking at Smoke or me, whispering and pointing. Nick was occupied with helping his daughter and friends dish up some food at the tables. Yes, I was a little paranoid.

The next few hours passed in a blur. I helped my mother keep the dishes filled with food and the coolers full of beverages. I introduced Nick to my mother, brother, grandparents, and friends. The sheriff stayed near my mother most of the evening, even helping her replenish food and beverages. He probably didn't know what else to do with himself.

Brian Carlson poked me when I was picking up some discarded plates and cups. "People asking you about the Molly case?"

I handed him a stack and picked up some more. "Yes, I've been cornered a few times. They can't seem to help themselves, can they?"

Brian shook his head. "First dismemberment case in our history. They want to know—but don't want to know—all the gory details."

"You got that right. What'd you think of the debriefing the other day? Did it help?"

He frowned slightly. "It did. Not that I'm overly interested in another dive any time soon."

"So did you burn your gloves?" I thought of the disturbed look on Carlson's face when he held Molly's arm and vowed to do just that.

"Naw. Bagged 'em up and threw 'em in the trash," Carlson said as we dropped our stacks of paper products in a garbage can.

"I'd have done the same thing."

"Mason and Weber and I all disinfected our wet suits about a hundred and fifty times."

I feigned surprise. "Is that all? I would have gone for an even two hundred."

My Grandma and Grandpa Aleckson, and Gramps Brandt were sitting together at a table on the edge of the dance floor. "How are you all holding up?" I asked.

"Hanging in there," Gramps said.

"I can give you a ride home whenever you're ready," I offered.

"No, no, I can make it 'til nine."

Grandma Aleckson reached over and patted my hand. "So, tell us more about that young man of yours. We haven't had much of a chance to talk lately."

I gave a brief summary of Nicholas Bradshaw. He was the Oak Lea Memorial Hospital Administrator. I met him while working on an investigation at the hospital about six weeks before. His wife had died of cancer, leaving him alone with a young daughter to care for, and to whom he was clearly devoted. I was the first woman he had dated since his wife died four years before.

"He seems nice, dear. Almost too good to be true." Her lips pursed with concern.

I half smiled and shrugged. "Maybe."

First Smoke then Grandma. I was beginning to wonder what they had against being "too perfect". Truthfully, I didn't know the depth of my feelings for Nick. I was attracted to him and loved spending time with him. He made me laugh. His kisses filled me with longings. His daughter was a treasure: polite, mature, kind, and—as an added bonus—she liked me.

"We saw your waltz with Detective Dawes. You two really cut a rug tonight." Both my grandfathers smiled with her.

I raised my eyebrows. "Cut a rug?"

"Old expression. Danced well, looked good together. Almost intimate."

"Oh." I dropped my empty cup on the floor on purpose. I hoped bringing blood to my face by bending over would cover my rising blush.

"I'm sorry if I embarrassed you, sweetheart."

I could never fool my grandmother.

Nick and I shared one last dance before he left. If he had any more questions about my relationship with Smoke, he didn't ask them. We held hands as we searched out his daughter and her friends.

"Faith, Janie, Sarah, we need to get going. Time to say goodnight," Nick prompted.

"Sergeant Corky, thanks for showing us your horses and for the fun party," Faith said.

"Yeah, thanks," twins Janie and Sarah said as one voice.

Nick made a gentle shooing motion. "You girls can get in the car. I'll be there in a minute."

They ran off. Nick led me out of the barn and drew me into his arms for a deep kiss. "Mmm, I've been waiting for that all night."

I smiled. "And it was worth waiting for."

"Can you come over later, after the party?" He squeezed my shoulders gently.

"It'll be pretty late by the time we get things cleaned up."

"Tomorrow?"

I exhaled audibly and shook my head. "Back to work tomorrow evening."

Nick frowned. "Oh, right. It's hard to keep up with your schedule. You ever think you'll work days?"

"I'm low man on the sergeants' totem pole, I'm afraid. Two sergeants either have to quit, retire, or get promoted for that to happen."

Nick nodded, then brightened. "I almost forgot–I did get those tickets for "Fiddler on the Roof" at the Orpheum in two weeks."

"Good! I'm really looking forward to it. It's been a long time since I've been to a play in Minneapolis. Years."

Buried in Wolf Lake

15.

Labor Day. The last unofficial day of summer. The weather was ideal–sunny, seventy-five degrees, no humidity. The perfect day to be on the lake swimming, fishing, or waterskiing, or taking a hike through the woods, or sitting on the deck with a good book, or digging in a garden.

Since my Grandma and Grandpa Aleckson had returned to Oak Lea from a month at their northern cabin, they spent as much time as they could with my Gramps Brandt. The Alecksons were in their seventies and enjoyed excellent health while Gramps' physical condition was deteriorating–not uncommon for a man in his upper eighties.

My mother was grateful for any assistance. She never complained, but between running her dress and accessory business, taking care of her own house, and doing a little volunteer work, caring for Gramps took the balance of her time.

My grandma and grandpa had an early tee time with friends, so I made a date with Gramps for the activity he most loved–fishing. We tried to get out at least once a week to one of his favorite spots in search of sunfish or crappies. Unfortunately, Gramps was losing his ability to walk. It was getting more and more difficult to get him in and out of the boat. I tried kindly suggesting places where we could fish from shore, or on a dock, but he preferred being out on the water.

We were all increasingly concerned Gramps would fall when he was alone and suffer an injury. He was determined to continue living in his house and the four of us were doing our part to help him.

"Hi, Mom. Hey Gramps." I kissed my grandfather's cheek.

My mother smiled at me as she set a plate of food

in front of Gramps. "Dear, I didn't expect you so early." Mom's hair and makeup were flawless and she looked especially pretty in a multi-colored, flowing skirt and silk blouse.

"I couldn't sleep. Cute outfit, by the way."

Her gray eyes twinkled with her smile. "Thank you. Just got some new things in last week and I fell in love with this skirt." She twirled around.

I grinned and poured myself a cup of coffee. "So John Carl got off okay?"

"He did." She added coffee to Gramps' cup. "I feel so bad for what he's going through with Emily."

I leaned against the counter. "Me too. He's already about the most serious person I know and this just makes it worse. I was hoping to spend more time with him, but man, the weekend went sooo fast."

She gave me a nudge. I shifted to the right so she could replace the coffee pot in its holder. "Way too fast. There is a silver lining, though. John Carl hinted if his marriage can't be saved, he is thinking of moving back home." Mom settled beside me.

I swallowed quickly. "I don't believe it! What did he say?"

"His exact words were, 'If Emily leaves me, there's not much to keep me in Denver.'" She shook her head. "I have been praying since he moved to Colorado that he would come back, and now if he does, it's because his marriage failed. I don't want that, either. You want your children to be happy and you want them nearby. If you can only have one of those things, which should it be? That's not a very fair thing to put on a mother, is it?"

I shrugged. "What is fair? Not what Emily's putting him through, that's for sure. But you're right, it's a double-edged sword. I guess if I had to choose, I'd go for whatever makes him the happiest."

She put her hand on my arm. "Of course. So do I."

I glanced at the progress Gramps was making on his eggs and toast. "You're raring to go after some fish, I guess."

"Are you hungry, dear?" Mom asked me.

"No, I grabbed an energy bar, juice, and coffee."

"I'll be finished here, shortly," my grandpa said.

"Take your time, Gramps. We are in no rush."

He took a last bite and slowly pushed his chair back, his hands positioned on the table to hoist himself up.

"It's these old legs of mine–they're all played out. I remember when your grandmother and I could dance all night. We'd a given you and that Elton fellow a run for your money."

Gramps, be quiet.

"What do you mean, Dad?" I envisioned antennae sprouting from the top of my mother's head.

A sly smile appeared on Gramps' face. "Well, the way they were dancing at the party had everybody at our table talking."

I am not here.

"Did I miss something?"

I checked the inside of my coffee cup. "I don't think so. You were there."

She reached over again and squeezed my arm. "I didn't see you and Elton dancing, so, according to Gramps, I must have."

Gramps was on a roll. "I always thought he might be interested in you, Kristen, but he was holding Corky so tight, we were kind of wondering how she could breathe." Gramps leaned back on his chair and folded his hands. He knew he had let a cat out of the bag and waited to see what would happen next.

Mother moved in front of me, her face inches from mine. "Corrine, there isn't something going on between you two–you and Elton–I should know about, is there?" Her brows furrowed tightly, producing a near uni-brow.

"No." *Nothing you should know about.* I was trapped against the cupboard and my only way out was with words. "Mom, on a related subject, I think it's time for you to fess up."

She straightened a little. "Fess up? You talk like

I'm one of your suspects."

I smiled. "That's not the way I talk to my suspects."

"Fess up about what?" I caught a hint of a guilty look. Very curious.

"How you happened to invite the sheriff to your party and why you two were acting pretty cozy."

Mother blushed slightly. "Okay, you might as well know. We've been seeing each other, a little."

"Seeing, as in *dating.*" A robin's feather could have easily knocked me over at that moment. I had never even put my mother and the sheriff together in the same thought.

"You don't have to look at me like that."

My eyes were wide and my mouth hung open. "How long has this been going on?"

"Um, I hate to bring up that horrible night when Alvie Eisner broke into your house . . . but . . . since then."

My hands flew up in the air. "Mom that was six weeks ago! I am your daughter, your neighbor. Twardy is my boss. I talk to you almost every single day, sometimes several times in a day. Why didn't you tell me? You haven't dated *anyone* in the twenty-nine years I've been alive."

She rested her hands on her hips. "This is exactly why I didn't tell you—you can get so riled about things, sometimes. I just thought I'd see how things went and if it didn't work out, there was no reason for you to worry about it." She turned to the table, picked up Gramps' empty plate then looked back at me. "And I've been out with men."

I shook my head and half smiled. "Mom, a few dinners—never with the same man twice—doesn't count as dating."

Her shoulders went up and down once, very quickly.

I stepped toward my grandfather. "Did you know about this, Gramps?"

He moved his head to one side and raised the

palms of his hands like he did.

I felt like a very poor detective. What giveaway clues had I missed over the past six weeks? I wracked my brain, but nothing popped up.

"Mother, I want you to start from the beginning and tell me what happened that infamous night."

"Now you *are* talking like I'm a suspect."

"Just talk. Please." I calmed my tone.

She looked away for a moment and sighed. "It was the worst night. There were deputies all over the place. I was trying to attend to you and Sara and clean up a little. I went to the kitchen to get something, and all of the sudden, it just hit me. I started bawling like a baby. I was so scared, thinking you . . . and Sara . . . could have been killed. Denny came in and put his arms around me and held me. I just felt myself relax and I knew everything would be okay."

I was transfixed.

My mother's face held a look of wonder. "It felt so good to be in his arms." *Okay, you can stop now.*

"Anyway, after that, he'd stop by the shop, bring me something from the deli for lunch. Or, when Stella was there and I could break away, we'd go somewhere to eat."

"I can't believe you–both of you–could keep it a secret from me. Who else knows?"

She glanced at my grandfather. "Just Gramps. We're taking things slowly, one day at a time. Denny's been through a lot you know, taking care of his wife when she was sick for those years, and–oh my–it was so hard on him when she died. He's had a lot of healing to do."

She looked at me for a moment. "Denny said the only thing that kept him going was his job. Oh!" She looked at her watch. "Job! I only have ten minutes to get the shop open." She bent to give Gramps a kiss and paused to hold me briefly. "Don't look so worried, dear. Denny is a good man." She kissed my cheek.

"Yes he is, Mom." That wasn't the point. The point was, how serious were they and what would it be like to have the Winnebago County Sheriff–my boss–as my stepfather, if it came to that?

We keep a lot of secrets in our family, I thought as I patrolled the highways and byways of Winnebago County in my squad car. Why would my mother date the sheriff behind my back? I didn't feel betrayed, exactly–more puzzled than anything else. And why hadn't I picked up any signals, any clues?

Admittedly, I had a number of secrets of my own. Maybe I was too absorbed in my own life to notice something had changed in my mother. And poor John Carl. He had been carrying the burden of a failing marriage around for months without telling us. Did he think was protecting us, Emily, himself?

Then there was Gramps. He missed my Gram terribly after over fifty years of marriage, but he didn't talk about it. When I told him how much I missed Gram, hoping to get him to open up, all he would say was, "We had a good life together." His failing health impacted his life, but he never griped about that either.

And Grandpa Aleckson was the king of silent stoicism. He didn't waste words unless it was for a good reason and personal issues were not good reasons. Grandma was the one I bounced my ideas and opinions off. She was the one who had defended my desire to go into law enforcement, the one who really understood me. She called me "My Heart" and I told her almost everything–with the recent exception of my confused feelings for Nick and Smoke.

Secrets, secrets, secrets.

My personal cell rang a little after five. "Hi, Sara."

"Hey! You guys catch any fish today?"

"We actually both caught our limits of crappies. I left the filets in Gramps' fridge–Mom will probably fix 'em when she gets home from work."

"She had the shop open today?"

"Yeah, she's says it's usually pretty busy on Labor Day. Teachers getting last minute outfits and accessories before school starts tomorrow."

"I s'pose. When are you taking your supper break?"

"I usually try for six-thirty–depends on any emergency, or being tied up on a call."

"Will you be around Oak Lea?"

I met a car with expired license tabs and did a quick U-turn to catch him. "I can be, why?"

"I thought I could eat with you."

"Of course, but that's a first when I'm working. What's up?"

I typed the license plate number of the suspect vehicle on my computer to do an owner search.

"We'll talk then. Why don't you come to my house?"

"Sure, but I only have a half hour."

"I know. Call me when you're a few miles out."

It was a safe place for a stop so I activated my lights to pull over the vehicle in question.

Sara set an omelet in front of me three minutes after I walked through the door and took my place at her table. I leaned over so cheese wouldn't drip on my uniform. "Mmm, this is good, thanks."

She sat down on a chair across the table, shook out a napkin, and dropped it on her lap. "We haven't had a chance to talk since the party and I can't stand it anymore–what are you going to do about Smoke and Nick?"

I chewed and swallowed. "Gosh, Sara, I really don't know. Just see what happens, I guess."

Sara waved her fork at me. "That's not like you. You're a proactive kind of person–"

"Who's not experienced in matters of the heart," I reminded her.

"True, but you must have some indication." Her green eyes were coaxing.

I took a break from eating and folded my hands behind my neck to stretch. "Sara, I honestly don't know."

She shook her head.

I rested my hands on the table. "I've known Smoke a lot longer and trust him implicitly, but Nick is great, too and I love his daughter. But don't forget, it's not up to just me."

"I know, but how long can this go on?" She threw her head back and groaned.

I shrugged. "As long as it takes."

"Okay, I'll quit bugging you–for now. Something else has been bothering me." Sara set her fork down and pushed her plate back an inch.

I studied her face for hints. "What?"

"It's your brother. I'm a little worried about him. I know I just met him, but I feel I know him pretty well after everything you've told me about him over the years. I think he's depressed." She paused. "At your mother's party, he was preoccupied most of the time. He'd start to relax, then a sad look would creep over his face again." Sara's mouth turned down.

I swallowed a bite and sucked in a breath. "You're right, unfortunately. His marriage is on the rocks. Mother said he might even move back to Oak Lea if they get divorced. I suppose that's weighing on him, too. Those are both in the top ten on the stress list."

Sara frowned and nodded. "For sure."

"The good news is, he's getting professional help, and Mother prays for him a lot."

Sara's frown turned into a smile. "Your mother is a treasure."

"My mother is dating Sheriff Dennis Twardy." I said slowly, emphasizing each word.

Sara's eyes flew wide open. "Shut up! How in the world did that happen?"

I awed her with all I knew about Mother and Twardy. We commiserated about the Molly case for a few minutes, then wound our way back to John Carl.

Sara stood, picked up my plate, and rested a hand on my shoulder. "I don't want John Carl's marriage to tank, but I have to tell you, I wouldn't mind if he moved back to here. He's really, really, really cute."

"Sara–"

"Just saying." She gave me a light slap on the back.

I pulled into Lake Pearl State Park, once again. I had taken many tours through there the past days. One week before a family's Golden Retriever made an appalling discovery that put everyone in the sheriff's department–and a number of area residents–on alert. I ran license plates of vehicles parked here and there in the reserve, and waved to hikers as they emerged from the wooded areas. There were two horse trailers, both longer than ten feet. Neither was hooked up to an Expedition.

Lake Pearl held the grandeur of an earlier day when it was part of what French settlers called "Bois Grand" or "Bois Fort." The English interpretation by the early settlers turned it simply into the "Big Woods." The park retained over 1,500 acres of the original 3,000 plus forest acres. Sunlight struggled to penetrate the dense masses of maple, basswood, elm, red oak, and tamarack. Red cedar grew on the banks of the numerous lakes.

Hikers, backpackers, skiers, and horseback riders loved to recreate in the park. Wildlife and bird lovers flocked to Lake Pearl in search of beaver, fisher, red fox, white-tailed deer, bald eagles, loons, hawks, egrets, trumpeter swans, and great blue herons. I did a visual sweep. Nothing in the park seemed ominous, or suspicious in any way.

My eyes focused on a basswood tree, its gray bark furrowed with S-shaped ridges. I visually tracked from its base to the tip of its tallest heart-shaped leaf, over one-hundred-twenty feet up. The tree had been standing at least a hundred years, perhaps as long as two hundred years. I wondered about all the things it could have seen and heard–if it had eyes and ears–over that span of time.

The forest was full of living creatures, but not one could give me information to help solve a hideous crime. Trees with branches bending in the breeze, animals scampering, loping, crawling, digging. All occupied with the basics of survival. Birds winging, singing, and perching. All potential, but mute, witnesses.

I turned into the Engen's driveway.
"608, Winnebago County," I spoke into my radio.
"608?" Jerry in communications answered.
"I'll be out at 8539 Abbott Avenue Northwest on a follow-up."
"Copy that, at 1930."

Tara and Dean Engen answered the door together, with Dean's arm tightly hooked around Tara's waist. They looked worried. No doubt they expected some news from me.

I smiled, hoping to ease their apprehensions. "Hi. I just stopped by to see how you two are holding up."

"Come in." Dean pushed the door open wider with his free hand.

"We were just cleaning up from dinner. Yes, come in," Tara offered as they stepped aside.

"I didn't mean to interrupt."

Dean released Tara and indicated a chair for me to sit in. "No, we're glad you stopped. We see squad cars driving by all the time now and wonder if there are any new developments—"

"And if somebody else is going to find another body around here," Tara blurted out as she sank onto the couch.

I thought of Amber Ferman, the Minneapolis prostitute who had gone missing a month before Molly. "I certainly hope not, but I understand your concern. No question about that. Unfortunately, there's nothing new to report. I know Detective Dawes talked to you, gave you what we know about the victim."

They nodded in unison. "If she's from Minneapolis, how did she end up here?" Dean asked as he sat down next to his wife.

I shrugged and shook my head.

Tara frowned. "What if it's one of our neighbors that did this?"

Dean enclosed her hand in his.

"We're conducting a very thorough investigation. I can't give you any specifics on that, but I can tell you we are tracking down every potential lead and checking out everyone within a specific area. If nothing turns up, we'll widen the scope."

Tara looked from her husband to me. "We don't know if we can stay here. Look at the beautiful day we had today. We didn't even want to be in our own yard. We drove up to the Sherburne National Wildlife Refuge to take Zeke for a hike."

I nodded to validate their plight. It was an awful situation having a dismembered body dumped in their small lake. It would squelch the desire to use the lake for any reason.

Tara paused a moment, then confessed, "I don't even like to go to bed anymore. I have nightmares."

I kept nodding. "That is completely understandable. You know what? So do a lot of the deputies. Me included." I put my hand on my heart. "Tara, you're the unfortunate person who got the first view of something very shocking."

Her lips trembled and one tear, then another, rolled down her cheek. Dean laid his hand on her thigh and squeezed tenderly.

I leaned toward them. "As awful as that was, if she–if Molly–hadn't been found, her family would be searching for her for the rest of their lives, wondering what happened. There would be no closure."

The sheriff's personnel debriefing jumped to mind. "I'd strongly suggest you get some professional help to help you deal with this. If you'd like, I'll talk to the chief deputy about a debriefing. Or, if you'd rather talk to a psychologist, we're lucky to have some excellent ones in our county."

"I think that would be good, the debriefing thing," Dean said and Tara nodded in agreement.

She looked at me, her face pinched with regret, or maybe it was sorrow. "Do you ever get used to it? The horrible things people do to each other?"

I didn't need to think before I responded. I had known the answer for a long time. "No, I don't. If I did, I'd quit my job on the spot. To be a good public servant you can never stop caring."

The sun was setting by the time I left the Engen residence. I pulled onto Abbott and headed south to continue my patrol. I was on County Road 10 when I met a silver Lexus with a burned-out headlamp going north. It was a slow night, so I swung around and activated my lights.

"608, County."

"608."

"I'll be out with Minnesota plate Two-William-Three-Five-Five-Sam at County Road 10 and Seventieth Street Northwest."

"At 2005."

As I approached the vehicle I was struck with a feeling that something was suspicious, hinky. It happened from time to time and reminded me to be cautious. From what I could see, the driver was the lone occupant. I quickly scoped the small backseat area. It was clean.

"Good evening, sir. I need your driver's license and proof of insurance." My right hand rested on my holstered gun.

The young bearded man behind the wheel leaned over and found the insurance document in the glove box, then leaned to the right and pulled his wallet from his back left pocket. There was a bottle of water in the seat divider, the only foreign object I spotted in the car.

"Do you know why I stopped you?"

"No, officer." His voice was strained and his hand shook a little when he handed over the documents. There was no odor of alcohol on him, and when he allowed himself a wary glance at me, I observed his pupils were even—neither constricted nor dilated. But there was something in his eyes that made me uncomfortable—distrust, or defiance, or was it disdain? Most people held eye contact when I spoke to them on a stop.

The man was clearly uneasy.

"You have a left front headlight out," I explained.

He glanced down and frowned.

"Is this your address current?" I moved the license a little.

His voice was weak. "Yes."

"Hamel. So where are you headed?" I attempted to sound casual, conversational.

It took him a moment to respond. "Ah, back home. I was at a friend's house for the weekend. He said this was the shortest way to I-94."

"Okay. I'll be back shortly."

I walked sideways to my squad car and caught the man watching me in his side mirror.

Langley Kenneth Parker: twenty-seven, five-foot-eleven, one-hundred-eighty pounds, brown hair, green eyes. Photograph and physical description matched the driver. Clean record, not even a speeding ticket. He was the registered owner of the vehicle. Not many twenty-seven year olds owned $60,000 vehicles. He either had a very high paying job or came from a wealthy family.

I debated whether to give him a verbal warning or a ticket, and decided to write a fix-it ticket. Parker accepted the papers and his driver's license. I told him he had ten days to make the repair. He read the ticket he held in his slightly trembling hands.

"Is everything okay?" I asked.

"Ah, sure. Ah, thank you."

For what? "Drive safely. There's a lot of traffic on the freeway tonight."

He nodded and waited until I turned off my lights to leave. I got weird vibes from people on a fairly regular basis. There was something wrong with that guy. Maybe he had a thing against cops, maybe he had a personality disorder, or maybe he had drugs hidden in his vehicle. But I had no probable cause to search his vehicle. I followed him for about two miles to make sure his driving conduct was safe, then whipped around and headed back south.

16.

A stupid headlight. He got stopped for a stupid burned-out headlight. As careful as he was to stay beneath everyone's radar–especially the cops–and his headlight burned out without his knowledge. It must have happened that day and it wasn't dark enough to notice the light was missing on his side of the car.

The cop noticed though.

A hot wave rushed over him, reminding Langley how much he hated cops. All authority figures, but cops especially. Every pulse point in his body hammered away. As the adrenalin continued to surge, his hands shook even more than they had when that female cop stood over him, staring at him. The unbelievable part of the whole thing was the cop wasn't a really a cop at all. She was an Eve dressed up like a cop. She crept up to his car like she wanted to find something so she could pull her gun on him–he was convinced of that. And she tried to sound tough besides. It was almost laughable. An Eve on a real power trip–the worst kind of Eve of all.

That was not laughable.

Langley saw the Eve-cop turn her car around in his rear view mirror. He pulled onto the shoulder to think for a minute and shake the remnants of adrenalin out of his hands. All he wanted was to drive past the burial site to savor the whole experience. She put a damper on that.

The Eve-cop wrecked it for him, filled him with doubts. What if she saw him driving past Wolf Lake, would she have stopped him there? Would he have somehow given himself away? But how? He was the only one who knew what was buried in Wolf Lake. He and Sheik, of course. He needed to gain his composure.

Langley patted himself on the back for making up the story about having a friend in the area. What if the nosy Eve-cop had asked where his friend lived, what would he have said? He spent enough time around there when he was a kid, and knew a lot of the street names to rattle off one of them. But, what if she asked for a name and knew what he made up wasn't true? Langley swiped his forehead with the back of his hand to remove the sweat beaded there. He rubbed the moisture into his jeans which caused a stir in his groin.

No time to get distracted.

Langley would not let the Eve-cop control him or what he did. He looked down at the ticket he had tossed on the passenger seat. It was signed by Sergeant Corrine Aleckson. She may call herself that, but she was just another Eve to him.

Langley continued to County 27. He turned left, then right on Abbott. When he crossed Eighty-fifth Street Northwest, he took a quick glance to his right to scan the path he and Sheik had taken out of the park, loaded with their cargo. His eyes fixed on the lake. Wolf Lake. A lake named for one of his favorite animals. Wolves stalked their prey and didn't give up until they got it. Wolf Lake would hold his concubine forever.

When Langley got home, there was a message from his mother.

"Langley! We got home from Vegas this afternoon and saw the Sunday paper. Why didn't you tell us what happened by your grandparents' old farm place? I am so glad they don't live there anymore. Well, we're off to dinner. Bye!"

Langley replayed the message. What was his mother talking about? His heart pounded as he made his way to a neighborhood store to pick up a paper. He went through the front section. Nothing. It was in the metro area section.

"Dog Finds Woman's Dismembered Leg. The Winnebago County Sheriff's Department reports a grisly discovery made by a family dog in Dayton Township. According to lead investigator, Detective Elton Dawes, the dog found the leg of a Caucasian woman in Wolf Lake which prompted a search of the lake. More dismembered

remains of the victim were found by the underwater recovery team. The victim has been identified as Molly Renee Getz, age 27, of Minneapolis. The dog's owners could not be reached for comment."

A dog! Dog, dog, dog, dog, dog, dog, dog. The word churned over and over in Langley's brain. His careful planning ruined by a dog. What a fool he made of himself by not keeping up with the news. He hated reading, or listening to news, and it had never once occurred to him Eve would be found. The lake was no good for swimming or fishing with its muddy bottom. In all those years at his grandparents farm, he had never seen one person use it, ever.

A dog.

It was the worst day of Langley's life to date and that said a lot. First, he was humiliated by the Eve-cop and then to find out Eve II was barely buried before she was found. He had failed. Wolf Lake had failed him. Maybe he knew all along something like that would happen. He didn't feel quite the same satisfaction with Eve II as he had with Eve I, as hard as he tried. He knew what to do. The only way to make himself feel better was to find another Eve.

17.

I stopped at the sheriff's office the day after Labor Day to talk to the chief deputy.

Kenner was standing in front of his four drawer file cabinet thumbing through a row of files in the top drawer. "Come in, Corky. What's up?" He pulled the selected file out and dropped it on his desk as he sat down to face me.

I sunk onto a chair across from Kenner. "I talked to the Engens yesterday and they are having a really hard time dealing with the Molly case."

He nodded several times. "Understandable. Very understandable."

"I told them I'd talk to you since you're so good at what you do, you know, with debriefing."

His eyebrows furrowed as his eyes searched mine. "They want a debriefing?"

I nodded. "I think it would help them a lot."

"I'll give them a call."

"Thank you, Mike." I released my breath, relieved the Engens would get the help they needed to work through their ordeal.

"No problem. I should have thought of it myself." He punched his right fist into his left palm. "In fact, I'll take it one step further."

He picked up his desk phone and hit a number. "Karen? I need a few things. First, check to see if we can get a conference room for a week from Thursday–that should give us enough time to pull this together. I need to contact a couple to do a debriefing. If they're free, we'll send letters out to all the neighbors out around Wolf Lake--invite them to be part of it, if they want to. . . . That's right. Thanks."

The chief deputy hung up the phone and slapped his desk. "Done."

The file on the Molly case had grown to about eight inches thick in a very short time. In addition to the report every deputy on the scene wrote, there were pages and pages of interviews with area residents. And Sergeant Olansky had sent the reports from the Minneapolis Police Department. I made a copy of Molly's picture and taped it to the inside back cover of the memo pad I kept in my breast pocket.

If the horror done to her was in the name of vigilante justice–someone targeting hookers–what led the killer to decide the crime of prostitution deserved torture, murder, and dismemberment? The things that happened to a prostitute on a regular basis were punitive in, and of, themselves. What had led Molly to work the streets? Abuse, drugs, money, booze?

I was reading over one of the neighbor interviews when I got a call from Ray Collinwood, the new Winnebago County Attorney. He had been appointed by the county board when Arthur Franz, the former county attorney, was killed by Alvie Eisner.

"How's it going, Sergeant?" Collinwood cleared his throat with a slight cough.

A loaded question. "It's going. How about you?"

I heard his office chair creaking under his substantial weight as he moved. "The same. Say, I just wanted to let you know we got the Alvie Eisner trial on the docket. Jury selection starts a week from Monday, the twenty-first."

I was taken aback. "Seriously? How did you manage that so fast? Two months from arrest to trial, that's almost unheard of."

"Let's just say we were very, very motivated. She got our boss, and you know how much we thought of Arthur around here." Collinwood's voice cracked with emotion. "We're slapping her with three counts of murder one, in addition to murder three for the going on thirty years-ago murder of her uncle, first degree assault with a deadly weapon, and so on."

A chill ran up my spine. I had stood on her uncle's grave under an oak tree, next to a swing, without realizing it. "I hope you can make the first degree murder stick. You should have no trouble proving premeditation."

"That famous word–should." Collinwood grunted.

"What are they doing about a public defender? Is it still that one from Sherburne County, the one who represented her at the first appearance and arraignment?"

"You haven't heard. Eisner hired a private attorney."

A *private* attorney. "She what? Who'd she get?"

"Ronald Campion."

"Ronald Campion. You have got to be kidding! He charges bucu bucks. How in the world can Eisner afford him? He's not doing it pro bono, is he?" I tried to envision Eisner locating, and enlisting, an attorney of Campion's stature.

Another grunt. "Campion? I doubt it, but could be for the publicity, I suppose. Maybe he thinks he can come up with something really creative to get a minimal sentence. Then he could charge his future clients even more than the immoral amount he gets now."

"Man."

"I found out in discovery he was looking at the insanity route, of course. Judge ordered two separate evaluations: one by a psychiatrist and one by a psychologist. They did testing, interviews, and both came up with–" I heard papers moving, "–Schizoid Personality Disorder–"

"Schizoid? Is that a form of schizophrenia?" I jotted the words on my memo pad.

"No, I looked it up. It's called an 'eccentric personality disorder.' People with it often appear odd or peculiar–"

"I could have made that diagnosis, if I'd known what it was."

"They avoid social activities, interaction with others–you know, they're loners. May seem dull or aloof.

Have limited range of emotions, so they appear apathetic--don't seem to have much sense of humor. They have what they call 'flat affect.'"

I made a list of the symptoms as Collinwood dictated. "Eisner could be the poster child for flat affect. No emotion in her expression at all. She has that perfected."

I heard him shuffling more papers. "The Psychiatric Society of America has criteria listed in their *Comprehensive Guide of Mental Disorders*. To be diagnosed with schizoid personality disorder you have to have four of the characteristics on the list."

"You have the list?"

"Yup, right here—I'll read it. 'They do not desire or enjoy close relationships, even with family members. They choose solitary jobs and activities. They take pleasure in few activities, including sex. They have no close friends, except first-degree relatives. They have difficulty relating to others. They are indifferent to praise or criticism. They are aloof and show little emotion. They might daydream and/or create vivid fantasies of complex inner lives."

I looked at the key words from the list I scribbled when Collinwood was talking. "From what I know about Eisner, I'd say she has at least four of those. So it's a personality disorder and not insanity?"

He let out a loud breath. "In her case, good question. The disorder is a mental illness, but so is depression—doesn't mean a person is insane. As you know, the insanity plea says the defendant is not guilty because they lacked the mental capacity to realize that they committed a wrong, or appreciated why it was wrong. Rarely, rarely works.

"Oh, I meant to tell you and we got sidetracked. The psychologist added another diagnosis—Post Traumatic Stress Syndrome. Must have gotten the incest by the uncle information out of Eisner."

I tapped my pen on the table. "Oh, great. That could add a whole new spectrum."

"I know. But, Campion agreed to the trial date, so

he must figure he'll have all his ducks in a row by then. I'm sure he'll call in expert witnesses. I should have his witness list by the end of next week. Why don't you look at your schedule and figure out a time when you can come in for a pretrial prep meeting."

"Will do. I'll check and let you know."

Alvie Eisner's trial would start in less than two weeks and I couldn't wait to put it behind me for good.

18.

Langley sat in the mandatory meeting while the director of The Veterinary Diagnostic Laboratory droned on and on in his soft nasally tone.

"We have invited key legislators from the Minnesota Senate Committee on Agriculture and Veterans Affairs, and their staff members, here for a tour this Friday. We're asking for an increase in funding from the state so we can continue to build our surveillance and emergency response. I don't have to tell you the importance of identifying the zoonotic diseases animals can pass to humans: tuberculosis, mad cow, avian influenza—"

Langley donned what he hoped was an interested face and tuned out. Maybe he could call in sick Friday. Maybe not. He hated the thought of making nice to a bunch of senators. On the other hand, he might need a personal day, here or there, coming up. It all depended on when he would find his next Eve. He was able to work the one weekday during the last Eve's capture. And it provided a perfect alibi—as if he needed one.

No one at the lab would ever suspect Langley had a secret life outside of work. When they asked him out for a drink after work, he always said he had to get home to his girlfriend—for one reason or the other—it was her birthday, they had dinner reservations, they were going out of town for the weekend—whatever he thought of on the spur of the moment. The other researchers and staff quit inviting him before long.

Langley could not banish the Eve-cop from his mind. She was always hovering in there, popping to the foremost of his thoughts, over and over. Maybe the way to expel her from his constant attention was to give her the message. The cops would never discover who buried Eve II in Wolf Lake, but they would know why she was there.

Langley had been convinced–with every fiber in his body–Eve II would never be found. And, by some fluke, she had been.

He needed to relieve his stress about the whole unplanned incident and develop a new strategy. If he left his Eves in places they would be found, it could serve as a warning to all the Eves of the world: use your power over men and you will be divided into pieces.

"–I think that's all. The tour starts at nine and will last as long as it takes. I know you'll all do what you can to answer any questions the senators have. Thank you. I'll let you get back to work."

The director was the first one out the door, Langley was the second. He made his way to the restroom and splashed cool water on his burning skin. His hours at the lab were precious. He had more important things to do than entertain senators to get more program money. Sheik was waiting for him to uncover the cause of Equine Cerebellar Abiotrophy, so he could find the cure.

Langley bent over the sink a long time, splashing water on his face. He needed to regain control and the brisk temperature of the water helped him think and plan. He did not want to look like a fool–like he hadn't planned for Eve to be found. Yes, the best thing was to send a message; play with the sheriff's department a little.

19.

I was still reading reports when Smoke stopped by the squad room.

"Corky, I just got a call from Sergeant Glen Olansky of Minneapolis Homicide. He's arranged a conference call with Special Agent Kent Erley from the FBI's Behavioral Analysis Unit in Quantico, Virginia."

I pushed my chair away from the table. "Seriously? When?"

"Tomorrow, 0800 our time. Any plans?"

"Outside of sleeping? Ah, no. This is way more important than sleep."

"No doubt. I'll talk to the sheriff. He'll most likely want to arrange for one of the larger conference rooms in the courthouse, get as many deputies there as possible."

The courthouse conference room was filled with deputies, in and out of uniform. All the brass were there: the sheriff, chief deputy, captains, lieutenants, sergeants. It was the first opportunity most of us had to be part of a telephone conference with Minneapolis Police Department Homicide and the Federal Bureau of Investigation's Behavioral Analysis Unit.

I walked in with Brian Carlson. There was a table in the center of the room with a beige telephone as its only adornment. Sheriff Twardy and Smoke hovered nearby. Chairs had been pulled into many rows of circles around the table. Brian took the last seat in the back row and I found one in the front. Smoke nodded his hello. Mandy Zubinski slid into the vacant chair next to mine, ogled Smoke for a second too long, then turned to me.

"Hi, Sergeant," she whispered.

My new best friend.

The sheriff held up his arms. "Okay, everyone, listen up! We've got the speaker turned up as far as it will go, but it's going to be hard for everyone to hear. The eighty or so bodies in here are going to absorb a lot of the sound. So hold your chit-chat until after the call."

At the appointed time, Smoke dialed the arranged number. After he identified himself and his department, Sergeant Olansky welcomed us and introduced Special Agent Kent Erley.

"Hello, everyone. Let's get right down to business. I've read through all the investigative information you sent, studied the pictures." Erley's voice was clean. He was a tenor with no frogs in his throat. I guessed his age at around thirty-five.

"Sergeant Olansky, you have two cases which may be related. Two victims, Amber Ferman and Molly Getz. Same general description–blond hair, just past shoulder length, average height, slim build. Both last seen working the streets on Hennepin Avenue in Minneapolis. Both disappear, unwitnessed–no evidence until the dismembered body of Ms. Getz was discovered four days after her disappearance in a small lake next to a state park in Winnebago County, approximately forty miles from downtown Minneapolis.

"According to the tests done at the Minnesota Bureau of Criminal Apprehension and the Hennepin County Medical Examiner's Office, Ms. Getz's body had been in the water for less than twenty-four hours. This would indicate she was held for three days by the unknown subject, or UNSUB."

The sheriff was looking at the phone and nodding.

Special Agent Erley went on. "Since Ms. Ferman hasn't been found, as of yet, we cannot say, positively, that the two are related. However, in reviewing the crimes from both a behavioral and investigative perspective, I would say they are."

Olansky's voice came across the speaker. "So what type of person are we looking for here? Someone targeting hookers?"

"Not in the way you may think. You're referring to a 'mission killer,' someone who is compelled to get rid of the 'undesirables' of society. The mission killer targets his victim, but there is no torture, no strangulation. He doesn't move the body after he kills her.

"This UNSUB despises women. To him, they are all bitches, whores. So, a component may be that they were prostitutes, but more likely it's because they are easy targets. He's punishing women because he believes they are powerful, evil. He needs to take that power away."

Mandy shivered next to me and we looked at each other a minute.

"You're looking for a sexual sadist. He's all about power and control. He rode on horseback to dispose of the body. He identifies with the innate power a horse possesses. He targets and abducts his victim, and takes her to a specific destination. He binds her, tortures, and rapes her and eventually strangles her. He records his activities, most likely videotapes them. He gets off on the suffering of his victim. His goal is to dominate and control. To him, his victim is a nothing. After she is dead, dismembering her reduces her to bits and pieces of nothing. Less than nothing."

There were quiet rumblings among the sheriff's personnel. We had seen the results of his brutality.

"What does he look like? His race, his age?" Smoke asked.

"On the surface, he's well-groomed. Good, or at least, pleasant looking. Caucasian. Intelligent, educated, middle to upper middle class. Twenty-five to thirty-five; lives alone, doesn't draw attention to himself. Most likely holds a good job. Neighbors would describe him as quiet, polite. Underneath the surface, he nurtures complex fantasies. He has a plan and he knows how to execute it. He's very methodical. And he will do it over and over again, as long as he gets away with it."

"Any thoughts on where a guy like that might live?" Sergeant Olansky asked.

"I'd say in the city, but he may have a place in the country where he can take his victims without being seen or heard. He either owns a horse or has easy access to one at, say, a relative's farm. The burial site he chose was not random. He's familiar with the area."

Smoke's solemn expression held my attention. He raised an eyebrow and sucked in a deep breath.

Erley's voice came over the speaker. "Let's take a look at the victims. Following the victimology on each woman, there is no evidence the two knew each other. According to the investigation the Minneapolis police conducted in both cases, Ferman had been in the city–on the streets–for several years. Getz moved from Kansas City to Minneapolis one week after Ferman disappeared, and three weeks before her own disappearance. Any attempt to link the two women to one viable suspect is futile. Their paths never crossed, according to what you discovered in your investigation.

"Sergeant Olansky, I suggest you go through your cases for the past several years. See if there are other missing women who match the victims' general descriptions. That is the commonality."

Olansky cleared his throat, but the gravel was still there. "Cripes, I can see some problems there. I mean, a lot of prostitutes leave the city without saying goodbye. Sometimes we get word through the grapevine they just get fed up with getting arrested and move on. Once in a great while there's a friend who thinks something is suspicious and reports it, but most times not."

"I'm talking about all women, not just prostitutes. And check with St. Paul, the metro suburbs. This guy is smart, meticulous. He did not plan for you to find his victim. He couldn't foresee a dog finding her leg and opening this investigation. And keep in mind, there could be multiple victims," Erley warned.

The sheriff leaned in toward the phone. "What drives a man to do something so vile?"

Erley's exhale was audible across the phone wires. "The question we ask a hundred times a day around here. A person can grow up in an abusive family and turn out okay. Another can come from a pretty normal family and be Jeffrey Dahmer or Ted Bundy. We just don't know why. I obviously wish we did."

"Is he a sociopath?" Smoke asked.

"Close. He's a psychopath. Both sociopaths and psychopaths can be very, to extremely, dangerous. They share a lack of remorse and pervasive disturbance of character traits, so there can seem to be some overlap between the two.

"A sociopath is usually from a more disadvantaged background, not as well-educated. He'll probably score lower on intelligence tests than a psychopath. A psychopath will come across as well-spoken, charming, maybe even charismatic. The sociopath will likely appear more unkempt, rough looking. Generally, a psychopath is from an upper-middle class background and he'll have a more clean cut appearance.

"A sociopath is impulsive. He takes what he wants, when he wants it, without remorse. If he wants sex, he'll rape. If he's angry, he'll become violent. He lacks impulse control. On the other hand, the psychopath is secretive, covert. He's careful, methodical–has an elaborate plan for the prey he's picked. It's all about power, control, humiliation.

"Because of their behavior, sociopaths are on people's radar. Psychopaths aren't, for the opposite reason. They are exceptionally careful, and experts at deception."

I had arrested several people who fit the description Erley gave of sociopaths.

"Oh, and I did run the info through our national database to see if there are any similar cases out there, but nothing came back. Any more questions?" Erley concluded.

The sheriff looked around the room, but no one uttered a word or raised a hand. Special Agent Erley gave us so much information, it would be a while before it sank deep enough into our brains to dredge up any intelligent questions.

Olansky spoke up, "Not a question, but I just got a piece of information. One of our undercover agents just got done talking to a streetwalker named Tasha. She got out of Ramsey County Jail last night and hadn't heard about Getz. She had talked to her a few times, but didn't really know her. Anyway, according to Tasha, she saw Getz getting into a tan four door sedan. No make or model or license number, and she was too far away to see the driver. She said it was about ten o'clock that Thursday night. We'll check again, go over some car models with her, see if any ring a bell."

The clear tenor voice was back. "That indicates brazen behavior. The UNSUB thinks he's smarter than we are."

Our bad guy had turned into a very ominous sounding UNSUB who thought he was smarter than the Winnebago County Sheriff's Department, the Minneapolis Police Department, and the Federal Bureau of Investigation.

20.

After two days off, I had a number of voice messages in my box. A woman wanted to know the status of the investigation on a burglary/theft case I was handling. An insurance company requested copies of a crash report. My third message was a man's voice that sounded like a computer-generated robot and uttered two words: "Judges nineteen." *What in the world? Did he mean nineteen district court judges or Judges 19 from the Bible?*

I pushed my wheeled chair to a nearby computer, logged onto the internet, and typed in "Judges 19." I clicked on the first selection. It was a King James version of the Holy Bible and the chapter was titled "The Levite's Concubine."

I began reading.

"1. And it came to pass in those days, when there was no king in Israel, that there was a certain Levite staying in the remote mountains of Ephraim. He took for himself a concubine from Bethlehem in Judah.

2. But his concubine played the harlot against him, and went away from him to her father's house at Bethlehem in Judah, and was there four whole months.

3. Then her husband arose and went after her, to speak kindly to her and bring her back, having his servant and a couple of donkeys with him. So she brought him into her father's house; and when the father of the young woman saw him, he was glad to meet him.

4. Now his father-in-law, the young woman's father, detained him; and he stayed with him three days. So they ate and drank and lodged there.

5. Then it came to pass on the fourth day that they arose early in the morning, and he stood to depart; but the young woman's father said to his son-in-law, "Refresh your heart with a morsel of bread, and afterward go your way."

6. So they sat down, and the two of them ate and drank together. Then the young woman's father said to the man, "Please be content to stay all night, and let your heart be merry."

7. And when the man stood to depart, his father-in-law urged him; so he lodged there again.

8. Then he arose early in the morning on the fifth day to depart, but the young woman's father said, "Please refresh your heart." So they delayed until afternoon; and both of them ate.

9. And when the man stood to depart—he and his concubine and his servant—his father-in-law, the young woman's father, said to him, "Look, the day is now drawing toward evening; please spend the night. See, the day is coming to an end; lodge here, that your heart may be merry. Tomorrow go your way early, so that you may get home."

10. However, the man was not willing to spend that night; so he rose and departed, and came opposite Jebus (that is, Jerusalem). With him were the two saddled donkeys; his concubine was also with him.

11. They were near Jebus, and the day was far spent; and the servant said to his master, "Come, please, and let us turn aside into this city of the

Jebusites and lodge in it."

12. But his master said to him, "We will not turn aside here into a city of foreigners, who are not of the children of Israel; we will go on to Gibeah."

13. So he said to his servant, "Come, let us draw near to one of these places, and spend the night in Gibeah or in Ramah."

14. And they passed by and went their way; and the sun went down on them near Gibeah, which belongs to Benjamin.

15. They turned aside there to go in to lodge in Gibeah. And when he went in, he sat down in the open square of the city, for no one would take them into his house to spend the night.

16. Just then an old man came in from his work in the field at evening, who also was from the mountains of Ephraim; he was staying in Gibeah, whereas the men of the place were Benjamites.

17. And when he raised his eyes, he saw the traveler in the open square of the city; and the old man said, "Where are you going, and where do you come from?"

18. So he said to him, "We are passing from Bethlehem in Judah toward the remote mountains of Ephraim; I am from there. I went to Bethlehem in Judah; now I am going to the house of the Lord. But there is no one who will take me into his house,

19. although we have both straw and fodder for our donkeys, and bread and wine for myself, for your female servant, and for the young man who is with your servant; there is no lack of anything."

20. And the old man said, "Peace be with you! However, let all your needs be my responsibility; only do not spend the night in the open square."

21. So he brought him into his house, and gave fodder to the donkeys. And they washed their feet, and ate and drank.

<u>Gibeah's Crime</u>

22. As they were enjoying themselves, suddenly certain men of the city, perverted men, surrounded the house and beat on the door. They spoke to the master of the house, the old man, saying, "Bring out the man who came to your house, that we may know him carnally!"

23. But the man, the master of the house, went out to them and said to them, "No, my brethren! I beg you, do not act so wickedly! Seeing this man has come into my house, do not commit this outrage.

24. Look, here is my virgin daughter and the man's concubine; let me bring them out now. Humble them, and do with them as you please; but to this man do not do such a vile thing!"

25. But the men would not heed him. So the man took his concubine and brought her out to them. And they knew her and abused her all night until morning; and when the day began to break, they let her go.

26. Then the woman came as the day was dawning, and fell down at the door of the man's house where her master was, till it was light.

27. When her master arose in the morning, and opened the doors of the house and went out to go his way, there was his concubine, fallen at the door of the house with her hands on the threshold.

28. And he said to her, "Get up and let us be going." But there was no answer. So the man lifted her onto the donkey; and the man got up and went to his place.

29. When he entered his house he took a knife, laid hold of his concubine, and divided her into twelve pieces, limb by limb, and sent her throughout all the territory of Israel.

30. And so it was that all who saw it said, "No such deed has been done or seen from the day that the children of Israel came up from the land of Egypt until this day. Consider it, confer, and speak up."

"Dear God!" I said out loud. I printed the chapter and headed to Smoke's cubicle. He was bent over a stack of reports.

"What's up?"

I tapped his shoulder. "There is something I want to you and the sheriff to hear and see."

Smoke pulled off his readers as he pushed back his chair to stand. "Whadaya got?"

"I'm not exactly sure, but it's not good." Smoke was at my heels when I knocked on the sheriff's door frame. He was writing in a file and closed the folder when he waved us in.

"Sergeant, Detective?" The sheriff looked from me to Smoke.

Smoke shrugged. "I'm just here for the ride."

I stepped forward. "I got a voicemail I want you to

hear. May I?" I asked, reaching for the sheriff's phone. He nodded as I dialed. I hit the speaker feature and the two words interrupted the silence.

The sheriff frowned.

Smoke nudged me. "Did you leave someone a message saying, where I can I find a good story and you got that message back?"

"I wish." I waved the printed chapter back and forth. "How well do you two know the Bible?"

"Truth be told, the New Testament better than the Old," Smoke answered and the sheriff shook his head.

"Dawes, read it out loud to save some time," the sheriff instructed.

Smoke slid his glasses from his pocket to his nose. He read the first line and commented, "Off to a good start. No king, in other words, no law in the land." When he reached the section on Gibeah's crime and how the Levite had dismembered his concubine and sent her pieces throughout Israel, I looked from Smoke's grimace to the sheriff's.

"For godsakes, *that* story is from the Bible?" the sheriff asked, the familiar reddish tint creeping over his face. He reached over and took the pages from Smoke.

"It appears so. Not all Bible stories are sweetness and light. There's always that battle waging between good and evil," Smoke answered.

"Hasn't changed much over the centuries, has it?" The sheriff drummed his fingers on his desk as he scanned the words of the chapter.

Smoke shook his head. "It seems there was no one in that story to bring the bad guys to justice. On the other hand, when we find our madman, we'll make sure he's brought to justice. Life with no possibility of parole."

I put my hands on the back of my hips and stretched. "Who is our madman, according to this story? Is he the Levite, the one with the concubine, or the men of Gibeah who abused her?"

"Maybe both," Smoke said.

"That's what it seems like to me," the sheriff

agreed.

"Is a concubine like a prostitute?" I asked.

"More like a common law wife," Smoke explained.

The sheriff leaned back in his chair.

I reached for the paper and scanned it, looking for the facts. "Okay, so his common law wife plays the harlot, the prostitute, against him. She leaves him, and he eventually gets her back. Then, to save *himself* from being violated, he lets a bunch of perverted men abuse her, which leads to her death. Then he takes her body home, cuts her up, and sends her parts throughout Israel. Everyone is shocked because nobody had ever done anything like that before. 'Consider it, confer, and speak up.'" I looked up from the paper. "Is he the one who killed Molly and this is his explanation why?" I asked.

The sheriff leaned forward and Smoke asked, "Whadaya mean?"

I lifted my left hand. "Just thinking out loud, here. We know Molly was a prostitute. We know she suffered torture and abuse before she died. We know she was last seen on the night of August twenty-first and her body—in part—was found on the afternoon of the twenty-fifth. The M.E. said she had been in the water less than twenty-four hours. So, you think electronic-voice man is both the Levite and the men of Gibeah?"

"I think that's a question for the FBI, the profiler, Erley." The sheriff continued to drum his fingers.

"There is something else I'd like to know," I said.

Smoke frowned in thought. "What's that?"

"I'm not the lead investigator on this case. You are, Smoke. My name hasn't been in any of the news reports. Yours has. Why would he leave a voicemail for me?"

The sheriff raised his eyebrows. "That is a good question."

"Could be cause you're the first name in the list of selections in the sheriff's deputies' voicemail box."

"Probably right," I said. But a sense of dread settled over me like a heavy blanket.

Smoke crossed his arms on his chest. "I'll talk to Sergeant Olansky in Minneapolis; either get Erley's number or relay the message and have Erley get back to us."

The sheriff nodded through Smoke's whole sentence. "He'll need to know—maybe give us some insight of what in the hell that message is supposed to mean."

"And, the BCA should do an analysis. It sounds like it's computer-generated. I'll have Darin pull it off your voicemail, Corky." Smoke blew out a long breath.

21.

"Are we all set for Friday night?" Nick sounded both expectant and cautious. I understood why. Things interfered with our plans several times in the past weeks, disappointing both of us.

"Yes we are, and I can't tell you how excited I am. I am almost desperate to get out of Oak Lea and Winnebago County for a whole evening." The crash report I was working on was sprawled across the table.

Nick's chuckle brought a smile to my face. "Maybe I should have sprung for a weekend getaway to somewhere more exotic."

"Minneapolis is just fine. I need to adjust to having fun a little at a time." I couldn't suppress my teasing laugh.

"Well then, we better make it a night to remember."

"I have no doubt."

"I'll pick you up at five and we'll get a bite to eat before the show."

Nick had been hinting he wanted to drive my classic, red 1967 Pontiac GTO. It had been my father's before his death and when my mother gave it to me a few years before, I had it restored to mint condition.

"Actually, I thought you could drive my car. If you want to, I'll pick you up."

He let out a "ha!"

"It will be a night to remember."

Between the Molly case--which loomed, ever-present, tugging at my mind and heart strings--and Alvie Eisner's upcoming trial the following week, I longed for an evening of fun and distraction.

When I steered into his driveway, Nick was leaning against his garage. His tall, fit body, adorned with a black suit, white shirt, and multi-colored tie, nearly took my breath away. And I was his date. It was almost too good to be true.

Nick waved. His grin was exaggerated, bordering on silly, and I giggled. I was barely out of the driver's seat before he swooped in and kissed me.

"She's all yours." I skipped around to the passenger side as Nick slid behind the wheel.

His knees assumed a frog-like angle.

"Whoa! I guess I need to move the seat back."

I laughed at his comical position. "I'm only like seven inches shorter than you."

His face beamed as he explored the front panel and carefully touched the buttons.

"You can drive a manual transmission, right?" I teased.

"I should have it down by the time we reach Minneapolis," he shot back. "By the way, you look particularly lovely this evening. I don't want you to think you take a back seat to your car." His grin spread to his ears and he reached over and patted my thigh.

I groaned. "Now, that is a really bad pun. But, thank you. My mother tells me a black dress is appropriate for just about any evening out."

"Your mother is right again."

"I'll tell her you said that."

"Good. I'm trying to win brownie points."

I squeezed his hand. "Like you need 'em with her."

After dinner at a trendy café in a brick, converted warehouse building, we stood in line outside the Orpheum Theater on Hennepin Avenue reading the "Fiddler on the Roof" posters, waiting for the house to open.

"I was in "Fiddler on the Roof" in high school," I said.

"You're kidding! So was I. Who'd you play?"

"I was in the chorus. How about you?"

"Tevya."

A tall, dark, very handsome Tevya. "So, you had your baritone voice as young as high school?"

Nick smiled a little sheepishly. "Senior year. The girl I stood behind in choir said I should try out for Fiddler. And, since she was also my girlfriend, I decided to give it a whirl. Only musical, only play, I was ever in."

"Seriously?

"Yup, and eventually I got the girl. It was Jenny," he added softly.

I moved my arm to his waist and squeezed. "You never told me Jenny was your high school sweetheart."

He picked at some strands of my hair. "The short version is—we dated my senior year, her junior year. I left for college, she went back to her old boyfriend. We met again when Jenny came to the same college. She was single again and we picked up where we left off two years before."

"True love found a way."

"Isn't that a song?" He bent his head and touched his nose to mine.

Musicals had a way of transporting me, uplifting me, and making me miss the days I had sang and danced in a few when I was in the high school drama club.

Entertainment allowed people to leave their workaday world for a couple of hours and get lost in make-believe. In my line of work, that was a welcome godsend. Oak Lea had an active community theater and if my schedule would permit it, I considered getting active, behind the scenes, if not on-stage.

We shuffled out of the theater with hundreds of others. Hennepin Avenue spilled over with people: theater goers, panhandlers, street people with their life possessions in backpacks, others playing instruments on the sidewalk to make a few dollars. As we walked to the parking garage, I scanned the nooks and crannies of the buildings and alleyways, picking out the drug dealers and the hookers.

"Hey. What are you looking for?" Nick asked, giving my shoulder a little shake.

"Ah, sorry . . . habit." I reached for his upper arm.

"See that red Saturn? Just pulled over to the curb? And that guy, see that Latino guy? He just pulled something out of his mouth and they did a quick exchange. Crack for cash."

"You should be a police officer."

I smiled and shook my head.

A young black woman walked over to a black Grand Prix. She leaned in the window for a minute, then got in. I wanted to call to her. Stop her. Magically change her life.

I scanned all the blonde women of average height on the street. Were they ladies of the night and potential victims of a crazed killer? I shuddered, feeling, believing, we were all being watched by *what*–I couldn't make myself think of the killer as a *whom*–the FBI called the UNSUB. With hundreds of cars cruising by, and as many people walking on any given night, where would they find him? Especially when half of the cars seemed to be four door tan sedans.

"Corky?" Nick's voice interrupted my thoughts.

"What?"

His brows furrowed in concern. "You stopped walking and I'm trying to steer you to the right. We're here."

"Oh."

Nick grabbed my hand and we maneuvered our way through the parking garage, dodging departing vehicles. We found my GTO on B-Level.

"Thanks for letting me drive this beauty. One of the highlights of the night." Nick brushed an imaginary piece of dust from the hood.

"You are very welcome. It needs to get out on the highway more often–too much around-town-driving. I was only mildly worried it would get keyed or schmucked."

"You're braver than I'd be."

On the way home we speculated about the personal lives of professional actors, some issues Nick faced at the hospital, and a little about the dismembered Molly. Molly. Her case had me in its grips and followed me, haunted me, wherever I went, whatever I did.

Nick pulled into his driveway. We piled out and met by the front of the car. "Come in for a while, or as long as you like. It's not often Faith is at an overnight." He drew me to his muscled chest.

I put my hands on his face. "You're leaving early tomorrow and I don't want to be the one responsible for putting a less-than-alert driver on the road, especially when you've got your precious daughter along."

He pulled me tighter. "I know you're right, but when I'm with you I want to keep you as long as possible." His kisses were coaxing, possessive, delicious, and tempting.

"Thank you, Nick, for the best time ever. And have a great time with the grandparents. Say 'hi' to Faith."

"Will do. See you when I get back?" He picked up my hand and kissed it.

"I'll be back to work Sunday afternoon."

"Ever notice how our schedules get in the way of our romance?"

22.

The last person Langley expected to see that night was the Eve-cop. He couldn't keep her out of his dreams. And she was on the arms of some john. A fickle concubine, no less. He stared at her for a long time before he was positive it was the Eve-cop. She looked different with her hair down, falling around her shoulders; tempting men in her little short black dress. Since she'd given him the ticket for the headlight, she'd been in his mind, day and night. He knew he would find her again when the time was right–he just figured it would have to be on her home turf, not his.

Maybe it was her home turf, after all. Maybe she worked for Winnebago County, lived in Minneapolis. Feasible. It wasn't far, maybe thirty-five miles to Oak Lea, the county seat. His grandparents had taken him shopping there a number of times over the years. Grandfather hauled his soybeans to the grain elevator in Oak Lea because they paid better than the one that was closer, the one in Little Mountain.

Langley pulled over to the curb and watched the concubine, the Eve-cop. She was like all the others, only worse. She put on a uniform and carried a gun to lord it over men on the one hand, then wore a sexy outfit as a different kind of power tool. Yes, the worst kind of Eve. He could imagine the way her neck would feel in his hands, her happy smile gone forever when he gained ultimate control over her.

Eve-cop and her john walked into a parking garage and drove out in a vintage car. She was still smiling. There was just no teaching some concubines. He had tried to warn her by sending her the message. He should have known she wouldn't understand how Judges nineteen applied to her, as well as all the other Eves.

He had the name she went by on his fix-it ticket

and would track her down. The online tracking services were reasonable enough and worth every penny.

23.

Instead of turning onto my road, I continued on to Smoke's. It was late, but I needed to talk to someone—someone who understood my obsession with finding Molly's killer. I pulled into his driveway. The lights were still on. His dog Rex yelped his "Oh, it's you, Corky" bark. I dialed Smoke's number.

"I'm decent." His voice held a mild slur.

I bent over to scratch under the dog's collar. "Hey, Rex. Good boy."

Smoke was sitting at his kitchen table holding a guitar in his lap. There were numerous empty beer bottles sitting in front of him. "Smoke?"

"You're looking mighty fine." He visually examined me, up and down. Twice.

I studied his lazy eyes and relaxed smile. "Are you drunk?"

"Pretty close." It was out of character and concerned me.

"What's up?"

"It's the one day a year I set aside to feel sorry for myself. The day I finally called it quits with Mona."

"I see."

Smoke was in love with Mona and wanted to marry her, but she wouldn't commit. After some years, he gave up, left his position in Lake County and moved back to Oak Lea.

"My brothers came over to help me—I don't know what—celebrate or mourn. A little bit of both." He strummed a chord on his guitar.

"So, you didn't drink all this beer by yourself?" I started to pick up bottles, counting and calculating alcohol intake.

"Leave 'em." He struck another chord. "What are you doing here so late? One of my brothers call you, worried about me?"

I sank down on a chair to his right. "No. Neither of your brothers has ever called me. Should they be worried about you?"

Two quick chords. "No."

I watched his long fingers on the guitar. "Good. You know what? It's nothing pressing–we can talk about it later." I started to get up.

"Tell me." Smoke rested his crossed hands on the body of the instrument.

I sat back down, slid a bottle over, and leaned my elbow onto the table. "It's the Molly case. It won't leave me alone. I just got back from Minneapolis–you know, my date with Nick–and I can't help thinking there's gotta be a way to set a trap for the killer."

Smoke raised his right shoulder a little. "That's up to Minneapolis. Could involve a whole lot of man hours."

"And well worth every minute to catch that animal and save a life, or who knows how many lives." I let my arm drop on the table and my fist bounced a few times.

"No argument here. But it'd be nice to have some sort of physical description, other than a general age range and that he's probably got a good job."

"True, but if we see a guy in the twenty-five to thirty-five age range, in a tan car, picking up a blonde, average-height prostitute, we could tail him and see where they go. I mean, isn't it a no-no to go to a john's house?"

"That's what they say."

"So, if he takes her to a private residence, we move in."

Smoke raised his eyebrows. "Corky, you know it doesn't work like that. We'd need a court order to do a search and no judge would grant one under those circumstances. Not enough probable cause."

"I know. I mean, ring the doorbell, see if he answers the door. If he doesn't, watch to see if he takes the prostitute back. If not, watch the house to see if he leaves without her." I picked up a paper towel from the table and dabbed at a wet spot.

"Two of the things I admire most about you are your dedication and your optimism." His hand captured mine and held it. "If I was in charge of the investigation at the Minneapolis P.D., I would assign you the detail. And, I will talk to Olansky, see if they have any kind of a sting set up. My thinking? An undercover cop would be the better approach. Damn dangerous, though and I wouldn't want you involved with that."

His hand slid up and squeezed my elbow. "Hey, forgot my manners—grab yourself a brew. You can help me with one last toast."

"And you're working on your *last* drink?" I dropped the towel and went to search the refrigerator.

"Yup."

We clinked the necks of our beer bottles. "Here's to . . . you think of something," Smoke said.

"Okay. Um. Here's to having someone to share your deepest concerns with." I smiled at my trusted friend.

"I'll drink to that."

Smoke downed the rest of his drink while I nursed mine.

"I gotta get rid of some beer." He set his guitar against the wall and left the room. At least he didn't stagger. Much.

I couldn't resist taking a load of bottles to the recycle bin by the back door. Rex followed me, as usual. He fetched a ball from somewhere and dropped it at my feet. I threw it to the other side of the kitchen then headed the same direction. Rex picked it up and started his mad dash back toward me the same time Smoke returned. Rex knocked against Smoke and Smoke stumbled into me. He clutched my shoulders to steady himself and prevent me from falling.

When he didn't let go, I looked up. A red flush had crept over his neck and face and the slight smile that pulled at the corners of his mouth dissolved as his eyes searched my face.

"The way you look in that dress is driving me

insane." His cheek brushed mine as his hands ran down my arms. "Ahhh, you smell almost as good as you look. If I wasn't half drunk, I'd be tempted to kiss you."

"Smoke—"

"I wouldn't want you to think it was the beer—"

Our lips were almost touching and I knew I should move away, but I couldn't. What was wrong with me?

Did you forget you were in Nick's arms, accepting his kisses an hour ago? I chided myself.

"Smoke?" I whispered.

"Ah, hell." Smoke's lips claimed mine and his hands massaged my back, urging my body so close it felt like his heart was beating in my chest. His kisses were exquisite, artful. I thought I must be dreaming. He gently nibbled around each of my lips, then followed with his tongue. When his open mouth came back on mine, I was barely aware my hands had moved to the back of his head, bringing him closer still, imploring him to deepen the kiss.

Smoke guided me backward, his lips on mine in kiss after kiss. We stopped and he tucked an arm under my thighs and lifted me onto the couch in his family room, then stretched out beside me. One arm was under me and he laid the other across my chest.

He raised his hand to play with my hair and face, then nipped here and there on my neck. I brought him in for another kiss, then did some nibbling of my own—his earlobe, his neck, and his chin, while his hand explored my body.

Suddenly, abruptly, Smoke rolled away and onto the floor. He pushed himself to a standing position and dropped his head into his hands. Losing his body heat gave me an immediate chill, but it took me a few seconds to sit up and get enough breath to ask, "Smoke, what is it?"

He reached down for my hand, pulled me up, and tenderly drew me into a hug. "Corky, we can't do this. Thank God I'm sobering up." A icy sensation ran through the veins of my body.

At that moment, I didn't care about anything except how much I wanted to be with him. I finally choked out, "Why not, why can't we?"

"A whole lotta reasons, not the least of which I'm almost twenty years older than you. We work together. Your father was my best friend. Your mother would kill me."

Smoke's words were cold water thrown in my face. My skin prickled and goose bumps rose on my flesh. I started to pull away, but he held fast. He hooked his finger under my chin and lured my eyes to his. There were unshed tears brimming on his lower lids.

Tears in Smoke's eyes.

The tears that had been building in my own spilled onto my cheeks. Smoke tenderly brushed them away with his thumbs.

"Corinne, you are the most beautiful, captivating woman I know. My humble apologizes for taking advantage tonight. Selfish desires got the better of me."

My anger and deep disappointment dissipated when he uttered "the most beautiful and captivating woman I know." I put my finger on his lips and shook my head. There were things I wanted to say, but couldn't. Not then. I eased out of his arms and made my way to the back door, escorted by Rex. I slipped out and drove home, struggling to see the road through the opaque veil of my tear-filled eyes.

Smoke phoned at nine the next morning, first my cell phone, then my home line. I let both calls go to voicemail. A few minutes later, Nick called. I let him go to voicemail as well. How could I tell Nick I had gone to see Smoke after our date? Yes, it was for a professional reason, but it got personal pretty quickly.

I laid in bed watching the ceiling fan swirl around like my emotions and reasoning, going round in circles, not getting anywhere. Would I ever be able to sort it all out?

Nick was the first man I had ever been serious

about, romantically. He believed I was afraid of commitment, afraid I would love and lose, the way my mother had when my father died at such a young age. Before he told me that, I hadn't thought of it that way. I assured myself I had just never found the right man to date.

Nick was carrying some heavy baggage of his own. He was widowed, with the responsibilities of raising a young daughter. His demanding career as a hospital administrator had him scrambling to make time for Faith, and for me. I loved Faith and knew I could help Nick fill in the time gaps when he was away, but could I be a good mother? A mother who didn't hover and over-protect to the point of suffocation at times?

Nick was intelligent, dedicated to his career, devoted to his daughter, and fun to be with--not to mention gorgeous. I felt like a celebrity on his arm, whether I liked that kind of attention or not.

Then there was Smoke. He had a whole room full of baggage. Or so he thought. After a long-term affair that was difficult for him to leave, he had moved back to Oak Lea to lick his wounds and build brick walls around his heart. He was interested in my mother until they had a date and discovered the spark they hoped for wasn't there after all. It was misdirected. I had to believe after our encounter the previous night, it was me he loved and wanted.

Could life be more complicated? It was no wonder I had shunned love most of my adult life. There were very good reasons to want to avoid all the problems it stirred up.

I threw the covers back and sat on the edge of the bed. My friend Sara liked to sleep in on Saturdays and it was a little early to call her. That left taking a run to alleviate stress and clear out some cobwebs. I pulled on sweatpants, a shirt, running shoes, and a hooded jacket. The autumn mornings had been cool lately.

Smoke was sitting in his SUV in my driveway. He got out, wearing casual clothes and a worried expression.

"I knew you'd come out for a run eventually."

"You know me too well." I pushed past him, dodging his arm when he reached out to me.

"Corky—Corinne—we need to talk." Smoke followed me down the driveway. "Will you stop for a minute?"

"No." I walked a little faster until I reached the road and started jogging.

"Are you going to make me *run*?"

"Suit yourself."

"Ah, hell. I don't know if I can run *and* talk."

"You don't have to do either."

For a few minutes, the only sounds were our feet hitting the gravel road and Smoke's noisy breathing. "Can you slow down a little? Do you have to go so fast?"

My pace was faster than usual, so I pulled it back, not enough so Smoke would be able to talk, but enough to help prevent him from having a heart attack.

After a mile of running in silence, Smoke passed me then stopped and pivoted to block me. We almost toppled over into the ditch.

"Geez, Smoke!" I pushed against his chest.

"I need a rest."

I gave his shoulder a light strike. "So take your rest and leave me to my run."

"This isn't like you. You aren't the 'silent treatment' type." His hands held my arms so firmly I would have had to use defensive tactics to escape.

I threw my head back and stuck my nose in the air. "Really?"

"Really. I need to explain some things to you." His eyes, the color of the sky overhead, held mine.

I was the first one to blink. "We'll talk at my house. Now, can I run?"

Smoke dropped his hands and I took off like a bat out of hell, leaving him in the dust. I ran another mile before I turned to head home. Smoke wasn't far behind me. A surprise.

A new Cadillac sedan cruised by. There was almost no through traffic on our rural road and I wondered if it was someone looking at the farm for sale a little way down from me. I waved and the man inside gave a slight wave back.

Smoke and I downed some water to re-hydrate.

"You want coffee?" I asked as I flipped the coffee maker switch on.

"I drank about a pot already this morning. Yeah, I suppose one more cup won't kill me. I quit wondering a long time ago what the inside of my stomach looks like." Smoke slid onto a barstool at my kitchen counter.

I stood on the opposite side. "You wanted to talk."

"Corky, what happened last night was–"

"A mistake?" I finished when he didn't.

Smoke shrugged. "Maybe. I was going to say 'inevitable.'"

I had to process that word for a while.

"We've been through a lot together in our years with Winnebago County. We have mutual respect, genuine caring for one another."

"Blah, blah, blah. Get to the inevitable part." I leaned closer.

"Because of what I just mentioned, and the fact that you are funny and beautiful and sexy as hell–when I was in a somewhat compromised position, like I was last night . . . I let myself get carried away–"

"–and now you regret it. Is this a 'Dear Jane' instant message?" I turned away and busied myself pouring cups of coffee.

Smoke moseyed to my side of the counter and picked up my hand. "No. I can't say I regret it, but it did serve to remind me of a few things."

"Such as?" His warm tone charmed me to look at him.

He squeezed my hand slightly. "Corky, I gave up on the idea of marrying some time ago."

"And?"

"You're very important to me and I'm not going to use you."

Lose me so you don't use me.

"Anything else?"

"There is. I hope you'll find someone to share your life with–get married, have kids." He took the coffee I had poured for him. "You know, Nicholas Bradshaw is not a bad guy."

"You said he was too perfect." My tone softened against my will.

"I did some checking and changed my mind."

"You ran a check on Nick?" I wasn't surprised.

"Didn't you?"

"Well, yes, but–"

"It's only smart. Corky, we have an excellent working relationship and we're even better friends. I don't want to screw things up by complicating it all. Can you understand that?" He set his cup down and rested his hand on my shoulder.

I shrugged, then nodded.

His finger hooked under my chin. "Will you answer me, truthfully, about something?"

"What is it?" I frowned slightly.

"How serious are you about Bradshaw?"

I glanced down for a moment then back at Smoke. "I think I could fall in love with him."

Smoke gently pinched my chin. "There you go. Do you forgive me for last night?"

I smiled with total sincerity. "There's nothing to forgive."

And I will treasure the memory of your kisses until the day I die, whether I marry Nick or not.

Smoke gave my nose a little tap and picked up his coffee cup again.

24.

Langley couldn't sleep. He should have located Corinne Aleckson the previous night instead of cruising for the next Eve. He tried a few search engines then settled on "The Online Sleuth." He skimmed over information he didn't need or want. All he needed was an address. Fifteen minutes of research produced a bonus– an overhead view of her house.

There was no inclement weather in the forecast. It was a good day for a drive to the country to find the concubine's–the Eve-cop's–place. He also felt compelled to drive by the burial sites of his first two concubines, even if Eve II wasn't there anymore. Maybe it wasn't worth the trip to Wolf Lake, after all. He recalled how energized he felt when he buried her. He'd hold onto that.

His parents were on a typical weekend away, so Langley would borrow one of their vehicles for his journey. When he was finished, he would return to the hobby farm to spend time with Sheik and go for a long, power-renewing ride.

A part of Langley was still in denial Eve II had been found. But he had kept the best part. He opened the freezer door of his side-by-side refrigerator. Eve I's head was on the top shelf, Eve II's was on the second. No one would find them there–ever. And there was plenty of room for more.

Langley stopped at his parent's farm in Hamel just long enough to greet Sheik, change vehicles, and stop by the private lake where Eve I was buried. He closed his eyes to savor his memory of the "plop" she made in the water when he buried her.

It was forty miles from Minneapolis to the Eve-cop's house. Langley was too preoccupied to notice much–about the small towns, or the fields of crops waiting to be harvested, or people darting in and out of stores doing weekend errands–on the drive between Hamel and Oak Lea.

Brandt Avenue was not what Langley considered an avenue at all. It was a gravel road in the country, just like the one his grandparents' had lived on. Their address was Rural Route 6 then suddenly it was Abbott Avenue Northwest when enhanced 911 changed the numbering system.

Langley turned onto Brandt, driving slower than usual to keep the dust to a minimum. He drove by Eve-cop's house. Way too nice for a concubine. He continued on to check out the neighborhood. By the time he reached the next crossroad, he discovered there were only two other houses on that stretch of road. Almost as isolated as his grandparents' farm had been when he was young.

He pulled over and sat for a full ten minutes, waiting to see how many vehicles drove down that road on a Saturday morning. Not a single one, from either direction. He waited another few minutes. Still no traffic.

Langley turned his car around for a last look at the house before heading to Wolf Lake. He spotted the Eve-cop running down the road toward him. His heart nearly stopped. He was scoping out her house and hadn't even hoped to see her. An older guy was a little ways behind her. It wasn't the man she had been with on Hennepin Avenue the night before. Another boyfriend? Her father? He noticed an SUV sitting in her driveway when he passed. It might belong to her; it might belong to him.

He recognized the guy after all. He was the Winnebago County detective the media interviewed the day after Langley got the message from his mother about the discovery in Wolf Lake.

If Langley could have vanished into thin air, he would have. Instead, he pulled his Twins baseball cap lower, so the bill rested on his sunglasses. He kept driving, right past them.

She waved at him! He had mere seconds to react and decided the only way for him to appear unaffected was to wave back. He lifted his pointer and middle fingers off the steering wheel in a closed-finger peace sign. It was the way his grandfather waved when he met neighbors riding in his truck or on his tractor. The detective glanced his way, but seemed distracted.

And out of breath.

Langley's hands relaxed their tight grip on the wheel. He had learned a lot on the journey to Brandt Avenue. Eve-cop went for morning runs, didn't have neighbors close by, and had virtually no traffic on her road. How did the detective fit in? Was he in some kind of training with her, or what?

He wouldn't worry about the detective. The Eve-cop's isolated road was a much better set up than Hennepin Avenue in downtown Minneapolis.

25.

I fretted all day Saturday and most of Sunday. I felt slightly better, for a while at least, having brunch with Sara on Sunday. Friday night, I had a wonderful date with Nick, only to end up in Smoke's arms, where we ventured into unchartered waters and nearly drowned. After two days of brooding, I finally recognized I was in mourning–grieving for a personal relationship Smoke wouldn't allow. True, I did have a blossoming relationship with Nick. And with Smoke's approval.

Jury selection was set to begin Monday morning for the Alvie Eisner trial and that gnawed at my insides whenever my head wasn't occupied with Smoke, or Nick, or the man who had brutalized Molly Getz.

In addition to the run with Smoke tagging along Saturday morning, I went for longer jaunts both Saturday afternoon and Sunday morning. The release I experienced running helped for a while, and then the doldrums would return to pull me down again. I knew who I needed to talk to, the person who knew me best. As I dialed the number, I prayed she would be home.

"Grandma?" It came out sounding weak, tentative.

"My Heart. What's the matter?" Her sympathetic tone choked me up a little.

I hesitated, then said, "I'm a mess."

"In what way, sweetheart?"

As I peered out my back window at the trees by Bebee Lake, I told her things over the phone I would be embarrassed to say in person–about ending up at Smoke's house on Friday, our near-miss and our conversation the next day.

It took Grandma a moment to form her words. "I have known Elton Dawes since your father ran around with him when they were kids. And I've known you all your life, of course. It was easy to see something had changed between the two of you when you were together at your mother's party. After I thought about it for a while, I realized what it was."

"What was it?" I stopped wandering around my living room and plopped on the couch.

"It was you, My Heart, it was you."

Not the answer I expected or understood. "Me?"

"Yes. Elton has always seemed to keep a pretty close eye on you and it's been obvious these last years you think a lot of each other."

"We do—we have complete trust and respect for one another."

"Yes you do. Corrine, remember, a couple of months ago you were excited because your mother was having Elton over for dinner. Now he's using his lovemaking skills on you. That's a pretty fast turnaround. Tell me what has changed." Astuteness was one of Grandma's natural talents.

I jumped up and started to wander through my house again.

"That's the other embarrassing part." I worked to squeeze the words out of my mouth. "I saw him almost naked—he was only wearing boxer shorts—and it hit me how attracted I was to him. I probably have been for a long time."

I caught my reflection in the entryway mirror and didn't immediately recognize my own face covered with a dark pink blush.

Grandma cleared her throat. "And that's what has changed, My Heart, the way you look at him. Elton has most likely been denying his attraction to you for many years. Then, when he saw that attraction mirrored in your eyes, he couldn't resist the temptation to do what he did."

"He wasn't alone in that." The feel and scent of Smoke overtook me for a second. "Grandma, what do I do now?"

I could see and hear Grandma's smile in her voice. "Elton is a wise man. Take his advice. See where your relationship with Nick leads to."

"You said Nick was 'too good to be true,'" I countered.

"So, if he's true, that's a good thing, right?" My very clever Grandma and her way with words.

"I love you very much, Grandma."

"And I love you even more, My Heart."

I didn't think that was possible.

Special Agent Kent Erley was out of the office for a week of vacation. When he returned, he contacted Sheriff Twardy and Sergeant Olansky in response to the two word–"Judges nineteen"–message I had received. He arranged a conference call for eight o'clock Tuesday morning with Olansky and his officers in Minneapolis, and Sheriff Twardy, Smoke, and me.

"Is everyone on board?" Erley asked.

The sergeant and sheriff responded in the affirmative.

Erley explained, "The UNSUB leaving this message tells us he found a new way to gain control of the situation. You were not meant to find the victim, but now that you have, he needs the ball back in his court. He has regained control by alerting the sheriff's department of the reason for his actions. He has taken the disturbing story from the Book of Judges and altered it to make sense in his own warped way of thinking and reasoning."

I looked from the sheriff to Smoke.

"And how is that?" Olansky's voice came over the speaker.

"He sees himself as a combination of the man who sacrificed his concubine to save himself and the men who abused her. The Levite's concubine left him and he went to bring her back. The concubine had a hold on him. Our UNSUB has deep seated issues with abandonment– either emotional or physical. Probably both.

"He hates the control women have had over him and how weak and ineffectual it has made him feel. He needs to sacrifice women he thinks of as concubines to preserve what he can of himself."

Smoke shifted closer to the phone to speak. "So why the message?"

"Unlike the Levite, the UNSUB did not mean for his victim's body parts to be sent out, to serve as a public message. But that has changed. His message is a warning. He has committed this crime at least once and won't stop. He can't. He sent the message to Sergeant Aleckson for one of two reasons: either he knows who she is, or he identified her as the first female on the list of deputies."

The sheriff coughed to clear his throat. "It's Sheriff Twardy here and I have a question for Sergeant Olansky. Sergeant, are you doing any kind of stakeouts?" he asked.

"I got undercover agents on the streets–mostly narcotics officers–but a couple working vice. They're keeping their antennas up for four door tan sedans, and Expeditions of all colors, involved in any suspicious activities."

Special Agent Erley spoke up. "The UNSUB is bold, but since he knows we know Molly Getz worked Hennepin Avenue in Minneapolis, he may look for his next victim somewhere else–another street, St. Paul. Prostitutes are easy targets, but, as I said last time, other women who fit his profile are also at risk."

When our conference call ended none of us moved for some time.

The briefings by Special Agent Erley were educational and very unsettling. We had learned a fair amount about the UNSUB's motivations, but we needed a lot more information to catch him. What did he look like, where did he work? Was it possible he looked and acted "normal?"

Twardy and Smoke and I silently studied our notes, then each other, for quite a while. The hush in the room was deafening.

"I don't like this one bit," Twardy finally managed. "Concubines, sacrifice, power, messages. As long as I live, I will not understand the twisted things the human psyche is capable of coming up with."

I thought of the Alexander Pope essay Smoke quoted the day we found Molly's body. Our savage criminal had embraced the "monster of frightful mien."

Smoke stuck his reading glasses and memo pad into his breast pocket. "I just hope Minneapolis can nab him if he attempts another strike."

"According to Special Agent Erley, it's not a question of *if*, it's a question of *when*," I corrected.

Jury selection for the Alvie Eisner trial took two days and went far better than either side had anticipated. Seven men and five women, from a variety of ages and situations of life, were chosen to hear testimonies and determine if Eisner was guilty, or not guilty, of the charges against her. The county attorney's office phoned to tell me testimony was starting the next day. I was a key witness for the prosecution.

The event I had dreaded for weeks began the same cool September morning I noticed reds, golds, oranges, and yellows infiltrating the green leaves of the trees.

A psychiatrist, and a psychologist, independently determined Alvie Eisner was competent to stand trial. The trial was open to the public, but no cameras or recorders were allowed, as per Minnesota law. Security was the tightest I had seen at the courthouse. Officers were posted at metal detectors outside the courtroom. They frisked individuals when they thought it was necessary. Inside the dark-paneled room, where the walls never seemed to reach the ceiling, uniformed and plain-clothed deputies were on the alert for potential vigilante actions.

The courtroom was packed and scores of people leaned against the back and side walls. Reporters were easy to spot among the spectators. I noticed a number of family members of the murdered victims and planned to check on them later, when we had a chance to talk.

"All rise! Court is now in session, the Honorable Wallace P. Feiner presiding," the husky bailiff announced.

The judge entered with another bailiff and took his seat on the bench. The stern look on his aging face deepened his wrinkles, giving the appearance of a scowling expression. Judge Feiner was kind, caring, and fair, but he threw the book at anyone who stepped outside the rules of the court, or showed any degree of disrespect.

Eisner and her attorney stood to hear the charges brought against her: three counts of Murder in the First Degree; one count of Manslaughter in the First Degree; one count of Assault in the First Degree; two counts of Assault in the Second Degree; three counts of Burglary in the First Degree; one count of Burglary in the Third Degree; and five counts of Felony Theft.

After opening statements by the prosecution and defense, County Attorney Ray Collinwood called witnesses and presented evidence as exhibits. After he finished questioning a witness, the defense attorney took over for his round.

Witness after witness testified. The psychiatrist, the psychologist, the nurse who smoked a cigarette with Alvie Eisner outside the emergency door exit, other nurses, doctors, Jason Browne, Sheriff Dennis Twardy, Deputies Brian Carlson, Todd Mason, Vince Weber, and Amanda Zubinski, Sara, Smoke, and me.

Eisner maintained her stiff-as-a-statue pose the entire time. She didn't speak and rarely blinked. Her lips pursed slightly from time to time then settled back to their natural downturn. The county attorney had given me the name for her condition: schizoid. By my observations, it seemed to fit.

My six hours on the stand were, without question, the longest of my life. I tried to look anywhere except at Eisner, but curiosity got the better of me time and again, and my eyes drifted to the woman who had tried to kill me.

The evidence linked to the death of Judge Fenneman included his IV tube with traces of the haloperidol Alvie had stolen from her brother's prescription; a piece of paper containing the code to bypass the emergency door alarm; a strand of her straight gray hair, retrieved from the hinge of Fenneman's eye glasses the night he died; and the note Eisner sent me after Judge Fenneman's death. The licked stamp and envelope contained her DNA.

Evidence from Arthur Franz's death included a soda can with traces of haloperidol; a sales receipt for a dryer hose and pillow, used to ensure successful carbon monoxide poisoning; his Palm Pilot, stolen from his vehicle; a 'suicide' note written on Eisner's computer; and a sheet of paper Eisner had used to practice Franz's signature.

DNA testing placed Alvie Eisner at Franz's death scene where she left behind cigarette butts and soda cans. Her work shoes were a perfect fit to the footprint cast taken at the scene.

From Public Defender Marshall Kelton's death there was a beer can with traces of haloperidol; his personal calendar, taken from his home; 'suicide' note written on Eisner's computer; and a sheet of paper where Eisner had practiced Kelton's signature.

Other pieces of evidence collected from Eisner's home were the three bullets missing from Jason Browne's home; two murder-suicide notes, one allegedly written by Jason Browne and the other by Sara Speiss, printed on the same printer as all the other notes. There were five pieces of paper, torn from one larger sheet of paper, each containing a name and description: Jason Browne, double-crosser, Marshall Kelton, useless public defender, Sara Speiss, spineless probation officer, Arthur Franz, merciless county attorney, Detective Dawes, heartless cop. Eisner's victims and intended victims.

My name was not on her original list—I had the misfortune to get in her way while doing my job.

A bullet, removed from Eisner's woodwork, was the same brand and caliber as the one found in the exhumed body of her uncle—the uncle she admitted shooting to defend her son when the uncle was assaulting him. Eisner had verbally confessed to the crime, but refused to sign a statement.

I lost track of the number of pieces of evidence entered as exhibits.

News crews hovered outside the courthouse, gleaning stories from any willing source. My voicemail box filled with request after request for interviews. I ignored all of them. One brave, not very bright, young male reporter was standing by my squad car when I walked out of a restaurant that Thursday evening while on duty.

"Sergeant Aleckson! KTLK news. Can you tell us any highlights of Alvie Eisner's trial?"

I kept walking to my squad car. "No, I can't. Please step aside."

"How does Eisner seem to be holding up?" He didn't move.

"Sir, if you do not step aside so I can get back to work, I will arrest you for disorderly conduct."

His chin dropped so low it almost hit his chest.

While I patrolled Winnebago County, my mind switched from the trial to the Molly Getz case. I zeroed in on every tan four door sedan, and all Ford Expeditions. I ran license plates until my fingers hurt from typing in the numbers. I jotted every plate number that came back to a man in the twenty-five to thirty-five age range to check on later, if I didn't have probable cause to stop the vehicle. It was my mission to find and stop the killer before he victimized another young woman.

26.

I was mentally drained and emotionally exhausted at the end of each day of the trial. Then I went on patrol for my evening shift and, in between the other calls, I obsessively looked for the man who had brutalized Molly. When Friday afternoon arrived, I was relieved to get a two day break from court and hearing all the sordid details of Alvie Eisner's crimes. I pulled over on the shoulder of a rural road and phoned Nick to check on our weekend plans.

Nick let out a loud chuckle. "Corky, it's good to hear your voice. This has been one long week at work. How are you holding up with the trial?"

"Let's just say, thank God it's Friday!"

His voice level dropped. "That bad, huh? Does that mean you could use a day of fun?"

"You could say that."

"All right! We picked the perfect day to head north tomorrow. The fall colors have reached their peak on the North Shore. And the weather promises to be sunny with temps in the sixties. If we leave at nine, we'll be in Duluth in time for lunch."

An oncoming car veered close to the center line, then back again. The wind was strong that night.

"Sounds fantastic. Did you check to see if Faith is interested in going to the aquarium up there?"

"She is. Oh, and Sarah and Janie are able to come along, too. I think one is more excited than the next."

I laughed. "They are such good little girls. See you in the morning."

Nick knocked on my door and called out before he entered. We met in the entryway. It was obvious we had both just showered. Our clean soap smells blended in a pleasant way when we kissed.

"I'd like this to happen every morning," Nick said into my lips.

"A wonderful way to start the day," I agreed.

"We have a car full of girls waiting for us." He stepped back and caught my hand.

"Hey, should we be embarrassed?"

"About what?" A puzzled look crossed his face.

I touched his chest, then mine. "We're dressed alike—jeans, blue tee shirt, navy hoodie, running shoes."

He looked at our outfits and chuckled. "Nah, we'll just look like an old married couple who likes to match their outfits."

"As long as the three girls aren't wearing the same things," I teased in mock horror.

"They are, but their hoodies are different colors, I think. Don't make me tell you what they are, though."

We were both laughing by the time we got to the car.

27.

Langley looked Thursday and Friday nights, but there was not an Eve to be found. He had no problem finding the others on the streets of Minneapolis, but he'd need to expand his search if one didn't turn up soon. He despised the feelings of helplessness and frustration. Working on his research project helped, but it only carried him so far.

Langley needed another Eve.

He crawled out of bed early Saturday morning, compelled to get another look at the Eve-cop. He knew she went on morning runs. Where could he hide so she wouldn't see him? His parents were home for the rare weekend and he couldn't borrow one of their cars without raising questions. He did have two cars of his own, though. The Eve-cop had stopped him in his Lexus—he'd take his Chevy.

Langley took a look in the mirror. Shaving his head and beard would change his appearance dramatically. It might raise questions among his co-workers, but why would they care? He could say his girlfriend liked the shaved look and asked him to try it. He rarely saw his parents, and by the next time he did, his hair would be growing back.

He started with an electric razor and finished with a safety razor. It took over an hour to do the job right. There were little red bumps peppered across his scalp and face; a little shaving lotion would help that. The change was startling and actually surprised him. Feelings of nakedness splashed over him, but he pushed them aside. He wasn't naked or vulnerable or exposed. He was Gideon. And Gideon had a sleek new look.

Langley decided on a quick drive-by past the Eve-cop's house. He parked some distance away where he could see when she left her driveway. If Eve ran in his direction, or another car happened by, he would take his car out of park and drive away.

The first hour of waiting passed very, very slowly. He had gotten there just after nine o'clock. Maybe she had gone on an earlier run that day. There was no sign of activity around her house at all. She could be gone, she could be sleeping. Langley wouldn't wait for her any longer. He'd head back to Minneapolis and hope for better luck finding an Eve there. Saturday night was a good night for prowling.

28.

After court on Monday, I was reviewing a report on a felony theft call I had taken when Smoke stuck his head through the squad room door.

"You're gonna wanna be in on this."

The intent look on his face brought me to my feet. I shuffled my papers into a smaller sprawl and followed him. "What is it?"

"A woman claiming to be Alvie Eisner's mother is in Interview Room B."

His words stopped me in my tracks. "No way! What planet was she hiding on?"

"You'll have to ask her that." He glanced over his shoulder at me.

"I'll let you do the talking."

"Feel free to chime in, if need be."

Smoke tapped his index finger on his lips, alerting me not to talk. He slipped into the observation area of the interview room and I followed. If I had given a thought to what Alvie Eisner's mother might look like, I would not have envisioned the petite brunette woman sitting at the table. Her eyes were closed and she worked her hands like she was rubbing lotion into them. The deep wrinkles on her face were likely caused by a life of struggle and worry.

I nudged Smoke and silently mouthed, "Eisner must take after her father."

Smoke inclined his head to the left, knocked once on the interview room door, and walked in, with me a few steps behind. He laid his notepad on the table and sat down opposite the woman claiming to be Alvie Eisner's mother. I closed the door behind me and leaned against it.

The older woman glanced at me, then focused on Smoke.

"I'm Detective Dawes and this is Sergeant Aleckson," Smoke offered as an introduction." The woman nodded slightly and frowned. Perhaps she knew who I was from news reports.

Smoke pulled out a notepad and pen. "The clerk at the front desk said your name is Elaine Van House."

"That's correct." Her eyes moved slowly to Smoke. She spoke quietly, just above a whisper.

"Can you tell us why you're here?"

Ms. Van House nodded. "It's about my daughter. She's on trial here."

"Alvie Eisner."

"Yes, I guess you knew that." She looked down at her vein-covered hands. "I was in court today."

That's why she recognized me—I had been on the stand for hours.

"I can't believe the things they're saying she did. I read about it in the Minneapolis newspaper, and then in court today . . ." She braved a quick peek at me and looked down again. "I can't imagine. I had to come. I just don't know what to do or what to say. I need to see my daughter, but how can she ever forgive me for leaving her, and her brother, Henry? I didn't go because I wanted to."

"Why did you leave them, and when was it, exactly?" Smoke's tone was matter-of-fact, accepting.

Her face was pinched. "I left because I was afraid, terrified actually. When? They were just little children: six and four. Alvie was six, Henry, four. Forty years ago."

"What were you afraid of?" Smoke asked.

"Of their father, my husband. And his brother." Van House pursed her lips.

"Why was that?"

She picked at the corner of the sweater she was wearing and began twisting it with her small fingers.

"Ms. Van House?" Smoke invited.

"Um, this is difficult. I've never said the words out loud before."

He leaned closer to her. "What words?"

"My brother-in-law raped me . . . more than once."
Ms. Van House watched her hands before braving a look
first at Smoke, then at me. Her eyes locked on mine. I
blinked and nodded, acknowledging her struggle. First,
living with the pain of her abuse and telling no one about
it. And then, having to tell two deputies she had met
moments before, a story she had never uttered out loud.
And one had testified against her daughter half the day.

I moved to a chair next to Smoke and placed my
arms on the table, palms up, hoping Van House would
relax a little and continue her story without our prodding.

"Go on," I said.

"I married young, barely eighteen. My husband
George was twenty-five. I thought it was kind of sweet at
first, how jealous he was, but by the time a few years had
passed, and we had the children, he was almost crazy
about it. I stopped going most everywhere so he wouldn't
accuse me of being with other men."

A story similar to a very many I had heard in my
years as a deputy.

Van House's fingers moved to her top two buttons.
She unbuttoned and buttoned them over and over and
over. I willed myself to not watch her compulsive
movements while we waited for her story to resume.

"George barely ever drank, but when he did he
drank too much and would rant and rave about how I
liked to lead men on, liked the way they looked at me,
secretly snuck off to meet them, on and on." Van House
closed her eyes and crossed her hands, laying one on
each shoulder.

"And then an awful thing happened. His good-for-
nothing brother lost his job and moved in with us. George
told me Albert would help keep an eye on me. That's
when the real nightmare began. George was . . . I guess
you would say . . . sick. Albert was worse. What man would
take his own brother's wife that way?"

Unfortunately, too many.

"Did you tell George about Albert?" Smoke
wondered.

"Yes, I tried. I mean, I did, but when he confronted Albert, of course Albert denied it. George believed his brother over his wife." Van House shook her head a few times. "Then Albert really had me over a barrel. He said if I ever said anything to George again, he would say that I had seduced him, and we had slept together."

"I can't imagine," I offered.

"No, I couldn't either, before . . ." Van House paused again. "George got worse after I accused Albert of the unthinkable. He threatened to kill me if he ever found me with another man, or if I tried to leave him. He had a gun." Van House shuddered at her words. "And I believed he would do what he said."

It was probably the same gun her daughter tried to kill me with. The one she had killed her uncle Albert with. I knew Smoke was thinking the same thing.

"Did he ever physically abuse you?" Smoke asked.

"He never hit me, but he did make me do things I didn't want to . . . things that hurt . . . um . . . sexually."

"Did you go to the police, seek help?"

She raised her shoulders slightly. "In those days?" She shook her head. "I didn't know how it would help."

Smoke nodded. "How long did this go on before you left?"

"About a year. When I started planning my escape, I knew I had to go alone. There was no way to safely get my children out of the house. As heartbreaking as it was, I had to leave them behind."

My mother would have taken a bullet in the back before she left John Carl and me behind.

"So I got up one night when George was snoring, grabbed my purse, and a small bag of clothes and personal items I had hidden away, and walked to a neighboring town, about seven miles away. We lived in southern Minnesota, about fifty or sixty miles south of here. They had a bus that made daily trips to Minneapolis. I paid cash for my ticket.

"From there, I took the train to New York where I lived and worked for over thirty years. When I retired two years ago, I moved back to Minnesota, but I never got up the courage to contact my children."

"Your husband didn't look for you?" Smoke asked.

"I'm sure he did, but it was easy to disappear in those days. George had the money to hire a detective." She shrugged. "I don't know if he got one, or not. I changed my name, got a Social Security number using a birth certificate I got from one of those underground operations."

"Weren't you afraid to leave your children with George and Albert?" I blurted out before I could stop myself.

"George had me convinced I was the problem. I thought if I left him, he wouldn't be jealous anymore and things would get better for the children. And Albert seemed to like them just fine."

If she only knew. Albert's abuse had caused irreparable harm to Alvie and Henry Eisner. Henry had spent his adult life in mental institutions and group homes, and Alvie had borne Albert's son—a son who lived outside the law and eventually died in prison by his own hand. It was a reality Alvie could not face. Instead, she blamed the legal personnel involved with her son's case for his death.

Smoke detected my growing agitation. "Sergeant, I know you have to get back to the case you were working on. I'll finish up with Ms. Van House, go over the info on Rebecca. Anything else you need?"

I had a dozen questions, maybe two dozen, I wanted to ask Alvie Eisner's mother, but what was the point? And it was clear Smoke thought it best for me to leave.

I was out on patrol when Smoke phoned. "Ms. Van House was both happy and sad to learn about Rebecca. She's over at the jail now, visiting Eisner."

I tried to imagine that scene. "I'm sure that will go well."

"So, what's your take on her?"

"She seems surprisingly normal. Aside from leaving her children, that is."

"I thought so, too."

"You think she'll seek custody of Rebecca?" I wondered.

"Who knows? She wanted to hear all about her. But, she's what, sixty-six? According to her D.L., anyway."

"Which is taken from a fake birth certificate," I reminded him.

"Ah, yes, the tangled web. She walked away from her own kids forty years ago. Would she want to pick up with a great-granddaughter at her age? I don't know."

"I don't either. That's up to social services and the courts, I guess."

I didn't believe Elaine Van House could be the stable, loving parent Rebecca needed to carry her though to adulthood, and beyond.

29.

Alvie Eisner's trial lasted a mere five days and ended on a Tuesday. The briefings, poring over records, listening to testimonies, giving testimony, studying the jury, watching the judge, and stealing glimpses of the defendant came to a sudden end.

Ray Collinwood rose and smoothed his tie over his ample belly. "Your Honor, the prosecution rests."

"Is the defense ready to proceed?"

Ronald Campion stood, his spine as straight as a planed board. "The defense rests, Your Honor."

The courtroom exploded with a hundred people speaking at once. I was too flabbergasted to do more than think, *What!*

Smoke was on my left side. He leaned over, squeezed my hand to get my attention and whispered, "What the hell? She hired a high dollar attorney for this? To *not* present a case? To not play the old battered syndrome card, at least?"

Before I could comment, the judge pounded his gavel and the bailiffs raised their arms, demanding silence. "I will have order in my court or I will clear the room!"

Order was regained in less than a minute.

"Mr. Collinwood and Mr. Campion, approach the bench." The judge spoke to the attorneys at a volume lower than the quiet din of the spectators. I glanced around the room, looking for Ms. Van House and saw her sitting a few rows back, across the aisle.

When the attorneys returned to their tables, they turned to face the bench, and continued to stand.

"Are the prosecution and defense prepared for closing statements?" Judge Feiner asked.

"We are, Your Honor." Collinwood nodded.

"Yes, Your Honor." Ronald Campion was stiff,

tense.

"Good. We'll take a fifteen minute recess." He tapped his gavel and we all rose with the bailiff's instruction.

Ray Collinwood rambled on for nearly thirty minutes, describing Eisner's actions, the testimonies, and the evidence supporting them. If I was a member of the jury, after listening to him, I would have no trouble casting my "guilty" vote.

Ronald Campion said little. "Members of the jury, you have heard the testimonies, received the evidence. Deliberate, come to a decision. We will respect that decision."

That was it.

I wasn't certain whether Eisner would be able to testify in her own defense. Given her schizoid personality disorder, it would be difficult for her to be questioned, and to give testimony—more so for her than for the majority of the population. But, like Smoke, I thought Campion would pursue the battered woman syndrome. Alvie and her brother had been sexually abused for years. It didn't make her less guilty of the crimes, but with the Post Traumatic Stress Syndrome the psychologist had diagnosed, it might prompt the judge to allow some leniency in her sentence. For example, being sent to a prison where she would be less likely to be harassed by other prisoners.

The jury deliberated for forty minutes. They filed back in, followed by the judge minutes later.

"Ladies and gentlemen of the jury, have you reached a verdict?" Judge Feiner asked.

The head juror, an older man of perhaps seventy, stood up slowly. "We have, Your Honor." He held up a piece of paper.

The bailiff retrieved it and handed it to the judge. After Judge Feiner studied the sheet for a moment, he instructed, "Read your findings to this court."

The jury found Alvie Eisner guilty of all crimes, except the manslaughter charge. Apparently, the twelve men and women of the jury believed Eisner's uncle got what he deserved. On a personal level, I didn't disagree.

Eisner and her attorney, Campion, looked like two wooden statues set side by side, listening as each charge was presented for the jury's finding.

"Ms. Eisner, you will return to this court for sentencing, on?" Judge Feiner turned to the court reporter for the answer.

"October eleventh at 9:00 a.m., Your Honor."

"Court dismissed!" A rap of the gavel ended the trial.

The sheriff joined Smoke and me.

"A helluva deal. Could have saved the taxpayers a load of money by pleading guilty in the first place instead of drudging up every unseemly detail at a trial."

Smoke scratched at his chin. "Yeah, I'm thinking something happened. Eisner must have finally decided all the cards were stacked against her, something like that."

Zubinski, Carlson, and Mason closed in on me and gave small hugs. Sara stepped in a minute later.

"I don't know how you did it, being on the stand so long. My own testimony seemed to go on forever," Sara said, wrapping an arm around my shoulder.

"Not easy, for sure."

The sheriff clasped his hands together. "You held up fine—all of you. It proves Winnebago County is lucky to have so many professionals on board."

Professionals we were and all of us were relieved the trial was oven, even with the abrupt, less-than-satisfying, end.

As the others filtered away, Smoke moved closer. "So, you still gotta work tonight?"

I nodded. "The chief deputy has my shift covered until five, so I'll use the extra time to work on reports."

"How are you feeling about now?" His eyebrows came together in concern.

I shrugged. "Numb, I guess. I didn't expect it to end like that."

"No doubt, kind of a shock all right." Smoke

leaned his head to the right. "Notice Van House is here?"

"Yeah, I saw her earlier." I glanced over at Van House. Her face held a bewildered, frightened look. "Well, I'm going to say 'hi' to the families, see how they're doing."

Smoke nodded. "Yeah, I see Clarice. Catch cha later."

I spoke with several family members of the victims. They had been on emotional roller coasters for weeks and could finally start dealing with the reality that the person who had killed their loved ones was held accountable, and would be punished.

I had one more detail to attend to. I had sent word to Alvie Eisner I would visit when her trial ended. There would never be a better, or worse, time.

I secured my sidearm and knife in a gun locker outside the jail, and pushed the call button.

"Can I help you?" the voice from central control asked.

"Sergeant Aleckson to see Alvie Eisner."

"Come on in. She's shackled and waiting in visiting room two. There's an officer posted right outside."

"Thanks." The first door unlocked and I stepped into the sallyport. When the first door secured, the second one opened. I nodded at Matt, the corrections officer standing guard, paused to gather my strength, and opened the door to face my attacker.

Alvie Eisner was sitting in a brown plastic chair about a foot back from a brown conference table. Her head was bent. Her eyes were cast on her hands which were cuffed to a belt secured around her waist. Being near to her—nearer to her than I had since our physical altercation—I realized she had lost weight over the past months in jail. I estimated ten or fifteen pounds. For some reason, I hadn't noticed it during court the past week.

Eisner's lifeless steel colored eyes found me when I stepped into the small room. I couldn't move for a minute and silently begged for bravery, grateful her feet and hands were bound.

"I didn't know if you would come." Her defeated tone matched her demeanor.

I remained standing on the opposite side of the table. "I didn't either. Why did you want to see me?" I sounded not in the least friendly.

"It's Rebecca."

"What about her?" My heart did a little *ping-ping* whenever I thought about Alvie's granddaughter, the little girl who was abandoned by both parents. Her mother left her on Alvie's doorstep when she was a baby and her father committed suicide not long after.

Her cold eyes leveled on mine. "You know I'll be sentenced next month—it will be for life. I'll die in prison." She spoke with certainty, then paused. "Rebecca deserves a good home, a good family. I don't trust social services so I'm asking you. I can tell you care about Rebecca and I'd like you to be in her life, to be her role model."

I was stunned, speechless. How could she ask such a thing? It was not a small thing by any means. It was a thing that would keep us connected, bound until death do us part. My legs weakened. I slid onto a chair and faced my attacker.

When I didn't answer, she went on, "I'm not asking you to be her mother, just her guardian." *Just her guardian.* "I want you to find her a good home. My lawyer has the papers. You'll get paid. There's plenty of money and there'll be more when the farm sells. A realtor told my lawyer it will get close to a million dollars with all the acres."

Still no words would come. She wanted me to be Rebecca's guardian. She would pay me to be so. And Alvie was worth over a *million* dollars. As she shared her plans regarding the sale of her farm, and finding a guardian for Rebecca, she seemed and sounded so *normal.* Alvie Eisner was anything but.

She shifted slightly on her chair. "I have no right to ask you for favors. That's why I want to hire you. You're the only one I trust to find her a good home. What do you say?"

What do I say? If you care so much about Rebecca, you should have thought about all this before you started killing people.

I finally found my voice. "Ms. Eisner, first I have to ask about your mother. Didn't she visit you yesterday?"

Alvie's hands strained against her cuffs, emphasizing muscled forearms and biceps. "I don't know how she can call herself my mother. I barely remember her, and she's about the last person I trust." She spit out the words with actual emotion in her voice.

"So you don't think she should be involved in Rebecca's care?" As her potential guardian, I had good reason to ask.

Her eyes narrowed. "No! Why would she show up now, forty years later? Maybe she thinks she's going to get the farm, or some money. Well she's not! She's been long dead to me and my brother."

I mulled over her words a minute. Ten-year-old Rebecca's lone caregiver faced life in prison. Rebecca must be devastated and scared to death.

I sucked in a breath of air before answering. "There is one thing we agree on–Rebecca is a very special little girl. I will do my best to find a good home for her, not for you, but for her. And I can't take any money for doing that."

There was a flicker of a smile, like a flash in a pan.

Her voice returned to monotone. "I understand. Thank you. My lawyer will be in touch with you. The money is all set up, so you should take it. It's not much."

Curiosity got the best of me. "This is a change of subject, but I have to ask you something. What happened today? Why didn't your lawyer mount any kind of defense?"

Another hint of emotion skipped across her face. "I wouldn't let him. The woman who calls herself my mother was there. My lawyer was going to bring up my whole past, going back to my childhood, and I couldn't let him do that. *She* has no right to know any more than she already does. After she visited me yesterday, I knew if Rebecca heard about everything, it would hurt her more. It wouldn't change my sentence much. If I had known she was going to show up, there would have been no trial. I would have pled—"

Alvie stopped talking and stared at nothing for second. Her eyes rolled back in her head and she toppled off her chair into a heap on the floor, her large body shaking convulsively. I had seen seizures in my career, but never on someone whose legs and hands were bound. The restraint belt restricted her jerking, handcuffed hands, and the leg chains banged and clanged against the metal chair legs and tile floor. I jumped up and scooted to her side of the table.

Matt stuck his head in the door.

I glanced up at his frowning face. "We need an ambulance."

Matt radioed central control, then dropped to the floor by Alvie and me. She was lying on her right side, unconscious, but no longer shaking. A strange combination of snoring and gurgling came out with her every deep, gasping breath. Bloody drool dripped from between her blue-tinged lips.

"Damn." Matt kneeled closer to Alvie and checked her carotid pulse. "It's racing."

"She have a history of seizures?" I asked, putting my hand under her head to give her better oxygen flow.

"Not according to her medical records here. I know she gets bad headaches; doesn't take anything for 'em. Just lays down with a cold washcloth over her eyes. One of the officers told the nurse, but Alvie wouldn't see her."

Two other officers rushed in to assist. "She's not faking it?" one asked.

I glanced up. "Afraid not."

"Should we leave her cuffed?"

"Yes. Cuffed and with an armed escort. I'll call the chief deputy." I would not be one of her escorts.

Sara opened her front door. "So you made the old bat seize up, huh?"

I shook my head and half shrugged. "She has a way of putting the fear of God into me, one way or the other, that's for sure."

"Into both of us. Are you kidding? When she had you in that death grip, I have never prayed so hard for anything in my life. What'd she want with you, anyhow?" I followed Sara to the living room and dropped onto her couch.

"You won't believe it—she asked me to be Rebecca's guardian."

"That nutso, who might I add, tried to kill you *and* me, asked you to be her granddaughter's guardian?" Her eyes were huge emeralds. "And you said 'no.'"

"Actually, I said 'yes,' which is why I'd like to have perhaps one final discussion with her about it. Maybe even arrange a visit between her and Rebecca."

Sara reached over and placed her inner wrist against my forehead. "I thought you'd be feverish. Have you gone off the deep end?"

"Short step," I quipped.

"Gosh, Corky! Okay, I have to say that you would make an excellent guardian for Rebecca, but she's *Alvie Eisner's* granddaughter." He voice rose a decibel.

"I know, I know."

"So tell me everything she said, exactly how it all went down." She settled back on her chair, her facial expressions changing as I gave my account of the meeting.

"If you weren't on duty, I'd offer you a glass of wine."

I raised my eyebrows. "If I weren't on duty, I'd drink two glasses. At least."

Smoke's vehicle was sitting in my driveway when I got home. I wasn't expecting him there at eleven o'clock at night, but I wasn't surprised, either. He followed me into my house.

"You could have just called," I said.

"I figured you'd hang up on me, or not answer in the first place," he countered.

"Who ratted me out?" I unbuckled and removed my duty belt, and laid it on my kitchen counter. It was fastest way I knew to lose five or six pounds.

Smoke hovered behind me. "I got back to the office after checking serial numbers on some possible stolen electronics at The Pawn Shop, and Mike Kenner tells me about all the excitement you had while visiting Eisner in the jail."

He grabbed my arm and turned me around. "Were you planning to tell me about it, little lady?"

I rolled my eyes and moved my head back and forth a few times. "Yes, but it could keep until tomorrow. Isn't it a little late for you to be out on a work night?"

He gave my arm a little shake. "I was going to let it go until tomorrow, but the more I thought about it, the more perturbed I got. What in the world would possess you to go see her?"

As exhausted as I was, it was easier to get the conversation out of the way. "I told you in the first place, I was curious."

He lowered his face so our eyes were at the same level. "And did you find out what she wanted, before she checked out on you?"

"I did." I pointed at one of the barstools. "Maybe you should sit down–"

He straightened up and crossed his arms on his chest. "I'm aging here."

"She asked me to be Rebecca's guardian–"

Smoke's hands shot up in the air, startling me. "Of all the lamebrain things I have ever heard! Well, that was an easy 'no.'"

Just tell him. "Not exactly–I agreed to it."

"You agreed to it. And why, pray tell, would you do that?" Sarcasm oozed around every word.

Sweat gathered under my bullet-proof vest. "I

could use a little support here, Smoke. I did it for
Rebecca's sake. She comes from such a dire background,
with health problems, besides. Eisner wants me to find
her a good home and doesn't trust social services. Okay,
don't laugh, but she says she trusts me."

"Oh, that is rich!" He let out a guffaw-like sound.
"With friends like that–"

"We don't have to worry about her anymore. She'll
be locked up forever."

"Thank the Lord. So how do you propose going
about finding a new family for Rebecca? And what about
Eisner's mother? How does she figure in?"

"I'm going to talk to Rebecca, see what she wants,
then to social services. Eisner does not want her mother
in the picture at all. It gets a little more complicated."

"How could it?"

I told Smoke about Alvie's fortune, the reason she
had refused to let her attorney render a defense, and the
details of her seizure. He was wide-eyed and silent
through my entire monologue.

"I'm about dead on my feet here," I told him
through a yawn.

He nodded. "It has been an eventful day. I'll get
out of your hair."

"Are you still mad?"

His long dimples deepened in his cheeks. "I
wasn't mad, just concerned. Okay, maybe a little mad."
His smile grew. "But I can never seem to stay mad at you
for long."

"A small favor?"

"What's that?"

"I could really use a hug."

"You're not going to try anything, are you?"

I had to laugh. "Just a hug."

Smoke held me for a long time. I calmed down
and felt emotionally stronger in his embrace.

"I bet you're itching to get out of your vest," he
said as he pulled away.

"That I am." I yawned again. "I think I'll sleep until

noon tomorrow."

"I'll do my best to put a hold on all emergencies requiring your attention until then."

"That would be good. Thanks, Detective."

"See you tomorrow, Sergeant."

30.

Langley was bent over his microscope when a large hand dropped on his shoulder blade. No one ever touched him. He hated being touched and startled in reaction.

Dr. Jones, the bald, middle-aged laboratory manager, held both hands up like he was under arrest. "Oh, sorry, Parker! I shouldn't have come up behind you like that. I just wanted to introduce the new lab assistant, Carrie Herman."

Langley's words caught in his throat. He had been looking for an Eve all week and suddenly, there she was. She had come to him.

The lab assistant offered her hand, "Very nice to meet you, Dr. Parker."

Dr. Parker, Langley thought, sardonically. Call me Gideon.

He wished his beard was there to cover his face, and the hair was back on his head. Eve looked at him with something akin to admiration, but Langley knew it was a ruse. She did it to make him feel unguarded, vulnerable. He pushed his glasses to the bridge of his nose and briefly shook her hand.

"Thank you."

"We'll let you get back to work, Parker. And I'll show Carrie around the rest of the lab. By the way, you look good shaved."

Langley nodded as they moved on. His heart was drumming so loud in his ears he thought his head might explode. He laid his hands on the table to steady them. All he could think about was how Carrie Herman's neck would feel in his grasp, and how her mocking blue eyes would change to marbles within minutes.

He would have to learn more about her: where she lived, if she lived alone, if she drove or took public transportation. He needed to find out without asking any questions himself. No one in the lab could ever see him initiating a conversation with her, or following her. He would eavesdrop–scrape together as much information as possible from chitchat and gossip.

A beautiful young woman in the lab was bound to generate interest. It was the way she worked herself into men's lives. It all started with the initial physical attraction. By the time she had power and control over a man, it was too late. For most men, that was. Not for Langley. He had figured out long before, the Eves of the world needed to be eliminated.

Langley couldn't wait to tell Sheik how an Eve had showed up at the lab. Like a gift. It was a reward for all the research and hard work he had done on the dreaded disease that had taken Sheik's brother and sister, and too many other Arabians. He would take Sheik for a long ride Saturday or Sunday. They both needed a power boost.

31.

The phone rang at a minute after twelve the next afternoon. It was Smoke.

"You awake?"

I was sitting on my couch, reading a magazine and sipping mint tea. "Yeah, like I thought I could sleep in 'til noon."

"Rested and ready for the next chapter?" His voice had an edge to it.

"What? A lead on the Molly case?"

"We could only hope. No, it's about Eisner. The sheriff got a call a while ago. She's got an inoperable brain tumor, hasn't got a lot of time."

"Oh, my God! I seriously thought the seizure was from stress. It was probably from the tumor. Poor Rebecca, poor little girl. What will I tell her?" I was overcome with an onslaught of emotions.

"Might be a blessing in disguise. She won't have to grow up writing to her grandma in prison, visiting her there."

"What kind of tumor?" I got up and started pacing.

"I don't have all the particulars. Just that it's fast growing and fatal."

I opened my entry closet door for no good reason. "Think it affected her judgment?"

"Good question, no clue."

I looked at my coats and boots. "Where is she?"

"Oak Lea Memorial. They brought a specialist out here so they wouldn't have to transport her."

"I was going to stop and see Rebecca after school. I better go see Eisner first." Whatever I was looking for in the closet, I didn't find it. I closed the door.

Smoke let out a grunt. "Here we go again. Okay, tell me when and I'll go with you."

"As my body guard?" I asked sarcastically.

"As your friend and supporter."
"Oh."

Alvie Eisner's legs were shackled to her hospital bed and her hands were cuffed to the transport belt around her waist. There were two deputies standing guard: Mandy Zubinski and Vince Weber. The sheriff was not taking any chances. I read genuine surprise on their faces when they saw us in the doorway.

Alvie had her eyes closed, a blanket pulled up to her waist. She opened her eyes and focused on me when I stepped in the room with Smoke. Her internal radar somehow announced my arrival. The woman was as eerie flat on her back, shackled to a bed, as she was lurking in a doorway, or sitting in a defendant's seat, or coming after me with a gun.

I was tempted to turn tail and run.

"I told you I would die in prison. It looks like it will be sooner than I thought." Her voice was raspy, quiet.

I nodded. "How are you feeling?"

She shrugged, appearing indifferent. "They give me pain medication for the headaches."

"How long have you been having headaches, Ms. Eisner?" Smoke asked in a smooth, melodious tone.

She stared at him a minute before answering. The detective she had intended to kill sounded like he cared. "A few months, they say, maybe four. They can't operate and it's too far gone to bother with chemotherapy or radiation. They call it grade four glioblastoma."

Ominous sounding.

"How long will you be here?" I asked.

"Not long. I'm waiting for the doctor to release me. They're making me take seizure medications with the pain pills. There's nothing else they can do." Her shoulders hitched up and down.

I didn't feel badly for Eisner, exactly, but I did feel badly for Rebecca and all the loss she had experienced in her ten short years.

I moved closer to the bed. "I'm going to see

Rebecca today. Anything you want me to tell her?"

"Tell her I love her." She must have read doubt on our faces. "I do," she murmured in quiet defense.

When Smoke and I stepped into hallway, Mandy Zubinski followed.

She spoke a step above a whisper. "The doctor has released her. We're just waiting for word from the jail. They're doing some shuffling so Eisner can have one of the small cell blocks to herself."

"Why's that?" Smoke asked.

"Mostly to keep her as quiet as possible. Another female or two in with her might get her agitated enough to do something to them. She's got nothing to lose."

Only her life, and that was quickly passing away.

On the way to our vehicles, I asked Smoke, "How much should I tell Rebecca?"

"I guess I'd ease into a bit. Start out gently, see where it leads."

"This is all so unreal. Last week Eisner had a personality disorder, this week it's a brain tumor. Between her case and the Molly case, I have learned more about medicine and psychology in the last month than I did in the whole last year."

"Not necessarily a good thing."

"No, it is not."

Rebecca had been staying with her best friend Tina's family. Dale and Jean Brenner applied to be her foster parents until legal placement became necessary. In addition to Tina, they had a son two years older than the girls. Jean and Rebecca met me at the door.

"Sergeant Corky!" Rebecca's face lit up and my heart melted.

I drew her to me and her skinny arms held on tight.

Three months before, she was so pale, blue veins were visible on her temples and cheeks, and there were dark circles under her eyes. The dark circles were gone. Her face had filled out and her skin had a healthy glow.

"Rebecca, you look great! And you've grown."

We smiled at each other, our own little mutual admiration society.

I followed Jean and Rebecca into the living room. It was simply furnished and comfortably lived-in. Jean indicated the couch, and Rebecca and I sat down together. Jean took a wing chair nearby.

Rebecca beamed. "I grew one whole inch since July."

"Wow, that is a lot. And I love your haircut." I reached over and tucked in an errant hair.

"Mrs. Brenner took me to a real salon. My grandma always cut it before."

Jean smiled at Rebecca's appreciation.

The mention of her grandma brought a little pucker to Rebecca's lips and her eyebrows moved together slightly. "My grandma's been in court since last week."

"Yes, the trial ended yesterday."

"What's going to happen to her? Why did she hurt those people? She never hurt me, or my kittens, or anything."

I reached over and picked up her small hand. "Rebecca, your grandmother has been sick for a while. That might have had something to do with it. I'm not a doctor—I don't know, but it might have."

"You mean like mental illness?"

Had she overheard someone talking about it, or read something?

I rubbed the back of her hand and spoke gently, yet firmly. "Your grandmother went to the hospital yesterday and they found out she has a tumor on her brain. Do you know what that is?"

She nodded, tentatively. "I think so. I had a kitty with a tumor on her leg. It was like a big bump."

"Yes. The bad thing is, when it's on the brain, it's not so easy to remove."

"Then what?"

"We'll have to wait and see. Meantime, there're

some things I have to tell you. First of all, your grandma said to tell you she loves you." I attempted another smile.

Rebecca's mouth quivered and her eyes filled with tears, which spilled easily down her cheeks. She sniffled and wiped them away as I went on.

"Your grandma will be going to prison. You know that, don't you?"

Rebecca nodded and tears continued to roll.

"I'm going to arrange for you to visit her. Would you like that?"

She nodded again.

"And–this is the exciting part for me–she asked me to be your guardian. Have you ever heard of that?"

She shook her head, "Uh, uh."

"It's someone to watch over you, protect you, keep you safe."

Her little flushed face brightened. "Like a mom?"

"In a way. Your grandma isn't asking me to be your mother–she wants me to find a good family for you to live with."

She looked down, considering. "Oh. Can I stay here?"

"You like it here with the Brenners?" I glanced over at Jean.

"Uh huh. I'll tell Tara."

I gave Rebecca a hug and she ran off to find her friend.

Jean moved from the chair to the couch. "Sergeant, we want to keep Rebecca. She fits in so well with our family. Social services had us fill out the child placement form. It's the same for foster care or adoption, and they approved us pretty easily. There seems to be no one else in her life, now that her grandma is going to prison."

"There are some things you should know." I told her about Rebecca's great-grandmother, the details of Alvie's tumor, and her upcoming sentencing. I decided not to share the part about Rebecca being a wealthy little girl– the attorney could handle that. It got me thinking. Was

Alvie's alleged wealth true, or was it a fantasy brought on by the brain tumor?

"I thought I'd save the news Rebecca has a great-grandmother for another time," I explained.

Jean lifted her elbow to the back of the couch. "What's she like?"

"Not even remotely like her daughter. She's pleasant, seems stable. But she did abandon her children when they were young."

"I can't even imagine." She paused in contemplation. "What do we do next?"

"I guess the first step would be to talk to Alvie's lawyer."

"This isn't very Christian of me to say this, but, I can't wait for Alvie to go away. Rebecca needs to be in a positive family environment. I'm sorry, but Alvie Eisner is a very strange woman. I mean, there was something about her that always scared me a little bit. I thought maybe she had some kind of social phobia, you know? But, we never imagined she could do anything so horrible. I mean, how could we? I look at it this way—we all have a choice in life and she chose evil over good."

32.

Evil over good.

Jean's words reminded me of the man I had planned to talk to for a while.

I pulled into the parking lot of my old country church, happy to see a car in the lot. I entered the side door near the back, where the pastor's office was.

Pastor Hobart met me in the hallway. He was an agile man in his sixties, with a kind face and hair of snow. He reached out and shook my hand.

"Oh, Corrine, it's you. I had a silent alarm installed so I know when someone comes in the back way. It's good to see you. What can I do for you?"

If he was surprised I was there, it didn't show.

"Do you have a little time?"

He put a hand on my shoulder and gently pushed me into his office. "Of course. I have a lot of it, in fact. Just working on some notes for Sunday's sermon."

We sat in comfortable leather arm chairs, in front of the south window in his office. The sun warmed my shoulders and neck.

Pastor Hobart was the first to speak. "You look like you are carrying the weight of the world on your back."

My lips turned up in a half smile at the concern in his voice. "Hardly, but a lot has happened in the past forty-eight hours."

I relayed the story of Alvie Eisner's mother turning up all those years later, of the trial and its unexpected ending, of our visit, her request regarding Rebecca's future, and my trip to the Brenner household.

"My, my, my. It's no wonder you're so burdened." He folded his hands in his lap. "But, if you need someone to give a character reference for the Brenners, I would feel confident to do that. My grandson is on the hockey team Dale Brenner has coached the last few years. Good people. And I know they're active in their church."

I agreed. "Rebecca seems genuinely happy there. And she looks so much better than she used to. They discovered she has a number of food, and other allergies, which were compounding her asthma. Knowing that, she can avoid the culprit foods, and take medications only when necessary."

"I'm glad to hear it. I'll make it a point to seek her out when hockey season starts, or whenever I run into the Brenners. She's going to need all the support she can get."

"Thank you, pastor." I hesitated before tackling the next subject. "You heard about the dismembered body found in Wolf Lake."

Pastor Hobart shook his head. "My, my, yes. An awful thing."

"I got a message from someone that just said 'Judges nineteen.' We believe that someone was the man who killed and dismembered the young woman named Molly."

"Judges nineteen." Pastor Hobart opened his Bible and turned pages to locate the chapter. "Ah, yes. Rather a gruesome tale, isn't it?" He looked at me and explained, "During the period of Judges, Israel had fallen into anarchy."

He flipped back a few pages. "Listen to what Judges two, verse ten says. 'All that generation also were gathered to their fathers; and there arose another generation after them who did not know the Lord, nor yet the work which He had done for Israel.'"

Pastor Hobart looked up again. "This is a common theme throughout Judges. When God allowed Israel to have its own way, do whatever the people wanted, things got bad. A judge was chosen to correct things, but then when he died, things would go south again. That cycle went on for a while, and the people kept getting worse. Every time a judge died, the people disobeyed in greater ways. At the same time, they longed for a king to get control over the rampant chaos. Ultimately, God was showing us there would be a king whose influence on us is eternal."

He read for a minute, his finger moving down the page, then went on with his explanation. "After the death of the concubine, the Levite rallies the tribes to war against Benjamin. It's a political thing.

"But the man who sent you the message—if he did such a wicked thing to a woman—he was not concerned about the underlying details of the story. He is caught up in the abuse and unspeakable acts against the concubine."

"It seems that's true. He is the Levite and the men of Gibeah all rolled into one lost soul."

Pastor Hobart stood and closed the book. "We fight the same battles, don't we, Corinne?"

"You mean against evil?"

He nodded, his white hair shining in the sunlight. "Yes. We just use different tools." He looked from the weapons on my duty belt to the Holy Bible he held in his hands.

33.

Langley drove his Lexus out of the university employee parking lot and pulled over to the curb near the front outside entrance of the lab. He lifted the notebook lying on the passenger seat and rested it against the steering wheel, then picked the pen out of his pocket and poised it in a writing position. If anyone from the lab saw him sitting there, they would think he had a sudden idea and pulled over to record it while it was fresh in his mind.

He waited about ten minutes for Carrie Herman to emerge from the building. She looked tired after her first day of work. There was a lot to learn in any new job. All Langley could think was, it was unnecessary effort, since she wouldn't live long enough to put her new skills to work.

The Eve, Carrie, walked to the end of the block and took a seat in the enclosed bus stop shelter. It was another seven minutes before the bus arrived. Good. Very good. When the time was right, when he was ready for her, he would offer her a ride so she wouldn't have to wait at all.

Langley followed the bus. When it made a stop, he continued to the next block, did a quick U-turn, and got back into position to follow it. The second stop, there was a place for him to pull into, one block behind the bus. The next time, he had to wait for a red light. All together, there were six stops and he was able to maintain his distance and blend in with the traffic.

Eve got off the bus on Cleveland Avenue and walked a short distance to a four-plex apartment building. Langley noted the number, drove a few blocks, and jotted the address of a random house in his notebook. When he asked Eve if she would like a ride home and she told him where she lived, he would tell her he lived a short distance away. Not out of the way for him at all.

A rag with a little chloroform on it would knock her out in seconds. It would be dark by the time they got to his warehouse loft. No one would notice a thing.

Langley felt Gideon rising to the surface again. Power and control were back within his reach.

34.

My grandparents planned to leave for their winter home in Arizona the following week, so my mother held their going away dinner on my evening off work. Mom invited Nick, but he had a meeting he couldn't beg out of. It was Grandma, Grandpa, Gramps, Mom, Sheriff Dennis Twardy, and I who gathered at the dining room table.

"Corky, we're not at the office. Call me Denny," the sheriff said.

It would be a while before "Denny" would roll easily off my tongue, but I was growing accustomed to seeing his car at my mother's house. He and my mother were both visibly happier and more relaxed. The sheriff's secretary commented, on more than one occasion, she was less worried about his health each week. He had even been able to cut back on his blood pressure medication. Where their relationship was headed was anyone's guess. My primary concerns for my mother were her health and her happiness.

"Denny, any new leads in the Wolf Lake dismemberment case?" my grandma asked when we took our cups of coffee into the living room.

"Nothing that has panned out. When something big happens–and you can't get much bigger than that–we get a lot of calls from people who think they may have witnessed something suspicious. Nine times out of ten, it's nothing. But it's always best to call in reports, cause you never know."

I wanted to lighten the timbre of the conversation. "Hey, I took a pretty unique call yesterday."

My grandma smiled in anticipation. "What was it?"

"A woman called because a two hundred and fifty pound pig was on the loose. It was in her yard two days in a row, eating the corn she had out for the birds and squirrels. She was afraid to let her children go out to play."

Gramps frowned in disbelief. "You took a pig call?"

"You never know what important task I'll be called to do next." I sucked in my breath and pushed out my chest.

"So what did you do?" Mother asked.

"Okay, don't laugh. I tracked the pig's hoof prints and saw they went west, then north."

Everyone was smiling by then.

"I drove to the next farm, about a half mile away."

"That pig really traveled," the sheriff observed.

I nodded. "It was a very athletic pig, I found out. I talked to the farmer/owner and he admitted he had trouble with that particular pig. He couldn't keep him penned. You were farmers–" I looked at my three grandparents and mother. "Have you ever seen a pig jump a three foot fence?"

"Of course not," my grandma said.

"Well, I did. When we were talking, that goofy pig jumped over the fence like it was stepping over a rock. None of the other pigs in the pen even seemed to notice." I giggled. "I wish I had it on video. All I could do was laugh and tell the farmer he'd have to figure out different living arrangements for the pig. It was one of the funniest things I'd ever seen."

Sheriff Twardy set his cup on its saucer. "We do get our share of animal calls."

"Yes, we do. That was my first involving trespassing and thieving by a hurdle-jumping pig."

Everyone laughed.

I stood up. "I'll do the dishes, then head over to Sara's. She rented a video for us to watch."

My mother made a shooing gesture. "No, just go. It'll take two minutes to load the dishwasher. And say 'hi' to Sara."

I gave everyone, except the sheriff, a hug. If I had thought ahead, I would have skipped the hugs altogether to avoid being rude. At least he didn't appear offended.

"Corky, you want some popcorn?" Sara opened a food cupboard.

I patted my stomach. "No thanks, too full."

"Red or white wine?" She held up the bottles so I could read the labels.

"Maybe red tonight." Sara pulled only one glass out of the cupboard and set it on the counter. "Aren't you having any?"

She shook her head. "I'm too tired. My caseload just seems to keep growing."

"Hey, we don't have to watch the movie tonight."

"No, I want to. I have to stay up at least until ten, or I wake up in the middle of the night and can't go back to sleep." She sat on a stool, plopped her elbows on the counter, and rested her chin in her hands. "So how is your love life going?"

I sampled the wine. "Mmm, this is good. My love life? Fine, I guess. Not that I see much of Nick, but we get along great when we're together. We are having dinner tomorrow night."

She lifted her head and stretched her neck. "Things been awkward with Smoke?"

"Not like I thought they'd be. We've been friends for so long—and almost lovers for not as long—so I try to keep things in perspective and try not to dream about him."

Sara's eyes shot wide open. "Corky!"

I shrugged. "Sometimes it's just hard to get your emotions to agree with your logic."

"Tell me about it." She leaned over and touched my arm. "By the way, I have a date."

I held my glass up in a mock toast. "Yay! Who with?"

"Casey Dey. You know, the Oak Lea officer."

"Sure. Good for you, Sara. Casey seems like a great guy."

"So how was the family dinner, with the sheriff included?"

I moved my head from shoulder to shoulder. "It's getting more natural. He's a different person away from work."

"Still seems strange—your mother dating anyone, much less Twardy."

"Tell me about it."

35.

I made arrangements with social services, the courts, the jail, and the Brenners to take Rebecca to see Alvie. Despite her terrible crimes, I believed Alvie loved her granddaughter. In her warped brain, she believed she was helping Rebecca, in some way, by getting revenge for her father's death. That was only speculation on my part, though.

Rebecca was dressed and ready when I picked her up after school on Friday. I admired how healthy and pretty she looked in her gray pants, plum turtleneck, and gray tweedy woolen jacket. Her cheeks had splashes of pink and her eyes sparkled when she saw me.

"All set?" I asked.

Rebecca nodded, a look of worry replacing her smile. "I'm a little scared."

"Of the jail? Of seeing your grandmother in there?" I guessed.

"Uh huh."

"Let's just concentrate on the positive stuff, okay?"

She nodded again and held my hand on the way to my car.

"I never got to ride in a car this old before, Sergeant Corky."

"Well, buckle up and hang on!" I kidded.

I helped Rebecca get situated in a visiting booth then took a seat in the adjoining waiting room. Alvie Eisner and her escort arrived a minute later. The officer locked Alvie into the inmate side of the booth. She put her hand against the glass and Rebecca mirrored her action. Alvie's face broke into a genuine smile and I was struck for an instant how attractive she was when she showed genuine, positive emotion.

They picked up their phones and I watched Alvie's face as she talked to Rebecca. I could read most of the words spilling from her lips. She told Rebecca she was sorry she had to go away and that she loved her. She said the sergeant would find her a good home. She said it would be the last time they could visit in person because children weren't allowed to visit in prison.

Rebecca's little shoulders quivered and I knew she was fighting to be strong.

The corrections officer unlocked Alvie's side of the booth, stepped back, and waited. Alvie made a kissing motion, mouthed "I love you," and slowly went back into the jail with the officer in tow.

Rebecca turned her tear-streaked face to me and I gathered her into my arms. I silently vowed to help make her life happy again.

"Sergeant Corky, my grandma says I can't see her anymore after today."

"I'm very sorry, Rebecca. That is a sad thing to think about, but we'll see if she can call you sometime, maybe write letters."

"She didn't say it, but I think she wants me to forget about her."

"I know you'll never do that."

And I won't, either. Unfortunately.

195

36.

Langley got through the week knowing he would get his reward at the end. He almost felt his control slipping a few times. He had to concentrate on the work he was doing for Sheik to bring himself back. Control was key to his continued success.

Several of the researchers got to work early on Friday so they could take off early in the afternoon. By four o'clock, the place was practically deserted. Fewer potential witnesses. The Eve-Carrie was scheduled until four-thirty. At four-twenty, Langley was in his car, ready and waiting, barely able to contain his excitement. He didn't want to appear overly zealous and scare her away. He needed to act calm and casual, maybe a little charismatic, to get her interested.

He overheard a conversation between one of the other researchers and the Eve-Carrie. She had moved to St. Paul to attend college and fell in love with the city. She lived alone in an apartment. A perfect arrangement. Hopefully, no one would miss her until she failed to show up for work on Monday.

If anyone happened to see him pick her up after work, he would, of course, admit to giving her a ride home. He knew where she lived and could give the address, if asked. He would say the last time he saw her was when he dropped her off at her building. An easy lie.

And no one would ever see her again.

At four-thirty-five, the Eve-Carrie walked out of the building and looked around. She spotted a car, smiled and waved. A fluke Langley had not anticipated. A man was picking her up–maybe for a date.

Damn. Damn. Damn. He had it planned so well. Everything was waiting for her at his loft. He put his head in his hands and rubbed the stubble that was starting to grow back on his head. Regroup. Rethink the night, the weekend.

There was nothing to do except to go cruising when it got dark out and the streets filled with harlots. He would find his Eve. He had to. In the meantime, he headed home to do some training and weightlifting. Gideon needed to stay strong and powerful.

Langley stared at the heads of the harlots, the Eves in his freezer, for a long time. He relived the ultimate high he felt dividing Eve I. Why was Eve II a let down? It didn't make sense. He would hit his stride again with Eve III and any disappointment he felt would dissipate forever.

Gideon would triumph once again.

37.

The early October sky was overcast and dreary. The brisk air carried a slight breeze that breathed across my face as I jogged down my road. Between the court trials I was scheduled to testify at–a domestic abuse, a criminal vehicular homicide, and a felony burglary–the Molly investigation, and my new guardianship, my brain was on overload. Running usually helped clear my mind and put things in perspective.

After I dropped Rebecca off at the Brenners the previous afternoon, I agonized about her future, and when and how I would tell her about her great-grandmother, the blood-relative Rebecca didn't know existed. She had her first chance at a stable family environment, but there were three women hovering in the shadows who had the potential to mar her happiness: her grandmother, great-grandmother, and her mother, the woman who left after her birth and was out there somewhere. I had begun to worry she would show up at some point in time and cause Rebecca more suffering and pain.

When I got home from work that night, I went immediately to bed, emotionally spent, only to toss and turn most of the night.

As I ran, questions kept popping up, one after the other. If I married Nick would I drive myself crazy worrying about Faith? If we had more children, what kind of a mother would I be? I wasn't a nervous person by nature, but I feared I would turn into a replica of my mother, the woman who had held an umbrella over John Carl and me all our lives. Mom was overprotective, hovering, to the point of being slightly neurotic, but overall, very good-hearted.

I was so lost in thought I didn't notice the disabled vehicle until I was almost upon it. It looked like a car I had seen on my road before. The trunk was open and a young man was bent over the driver's side back tire. He stood and turned to me. There was something familiar about him. Before I could speak or react, he raised his arm. I saw a flash of metal before I felt the blow. Everything went black.

38.

He wasn't able to gag her or tie her up. A tractor pulling a hay wagon came down the road toward him. All he could do was throw her in the trunk and close it before she was seen. It shouldn't be a problem–she should be unconscious for a long, long time. He didn't want to kill her; that would spoil the fun. He just needed to transport her, first to Hamel, then to his Minneapolis loft.

Langley hadn't figured on any traffic on the rural road, so the tractor was a big surprise. He abhorred the unexpected. The last times he had been on Brandt Avenue, there wasn't a car, or truck, or bicycle, or other moving vehicle in sight. He couldn't obsess about it. The rest of his plans would flow smoothly.

He was Gideon and Gideon would gain ultimate control of the Eve-cop. All the power she wielded would end. She was a worse kind of Eve than the others. The Eve-cop not only dressed up in sexy outfits to tempt men, she also put on her cop uniform, and drove a squad car, and pulled people over for stupid things like a burned-out headlight. Her false sense of authority and control was about to end.

Langley met a Winnebago County squad car. He smirked when it drove past him. The sooner he got out of the county, the better. He couldn't take any chances of getting stopped for speeding, so he willed himself to calm down and enjoy the ride.

His reward would begin that night.

There was a crash on County Road 35. It appeared a car had attempted a left turn in front of another car and hadn't made it. Lights from squad cars and an ambulance lit up the scene. It didn't look very serious, but traffic was halted while the crashed vehicles were loaded onto flatbed trailers. Langley was tempted to turn around and find another route, but that might be the slower option. Take deep breaths, he told himself, over and over. It was almost time for his next reward.

39.

I became aware of things in a fog, or maybe it was a dream. I kept pushing to wake up. It was dark and I was moving. How could I be lying there and be in motion?

I hurt.

It was the side of my head that hurt the most. I slid my arm up, and gently probed my skull with my hand. I had a bump on the side of my head. I tried to open my left eye, but it wouldn't budge. There was a buzzing sound in my ears. Something smelled bad, like rubber and metal and dirt and gasoline, all mixed together. And why would I be lying down in such a place? If I wasn't dreaming, then I must have gotten injured somehow.

The last thing I remembered was running down my road. Maybe I got struck by a vehicle. Was I in an ambulance? If only I could think!

"Hello?" My voice didn't sound like my own. "Hello? Is anybody there?"

No answer. I heard road sounds. I was in a moving vehicle. Why?

My right arm was the only part of me I could move and I patted places on my body within reach, to see if anything was broken or bleeding. My hand rested on something hard. It was the cell phone I had stuck in my inside pants pocket. Maybe if I called someone they would know where I was going.

I was finally able to move my left leg. I stretched it out, then bent my knee and turned it upward. It touched a low ceiling of something hard and cold. Metal.

I was in the trunk of a car!

Smoke answered on the second ring. "Morning, Corky."

"Smoke . . ."

"Corky, what's wrong? Are you crying?"

"Um, um, I'm in trouble."

His voice held an edge of urgency. "What happened? Where are you?"

"I don't know what happened, but I'm in the trunk of a car and it's moving. I don't know why. I just woke up."

"Corky! You're in the *trunk of a moving car* and you don't know why!" Smoke's rapid breathing sounded like he was running. I heard him suck in a deep breath. "Okay, let's talk this through. What is the last thing you remember before you fell asleep? Were you in your bed?" His voice had calmed, I suspected for my benefit.

I remembered. "No, I was on a run."

"Okay, good. You were on a run. Where?"

"On Brandt. I'm trying to think. Um, maybe a half mile from my house."

"East or west?"

It took me a minute to process the concept of direction. "East."

"Good. What time was that?"

"Time." I had checked my watch at the end of my driveway. I envisioned looking at the face of my cell phone before I stuck it in my pocket. "It was nine-eleven when I left, so about nine-fourteen."

"It's nine-thirty now. What happened next?" he coaxed.

"That's the really fuzzy part." My brain was clearing slightly. "Oh, yeah. There was a car, a Cadillac, one I'd seen before, on the side of the road in front of me."

"Also facing east?"

I remembered seeing the open trunk. "Yes."

"What was it doing there?"

"Well, I think the driver was changing the tire. Or checking the tire. I'm not sure. Wait! Now I remember! I was going to see if he needed help and I think he hit me on the head with something. I remember seeing a flash and the next thing I knew I was in here."

"You've been kidnapped?" Smoke's voice was shaky.

"Oh, God!" My heart pounded so hard, I thought it

would break through my chest. Terror stabbed me, invaded my body, and struck all the way down to my bone marrow.

His voiced cracked. "What did he look like?"

Focus, Corky. "Youngish. Thirty, maybe. Shaved head. Familiar."

"How so?"

Someone I had arrested? Someone I had seen at the grocery store? "I just don't remember."

Smoke coughed. "We will find you; I promise you that. Vehicle color?"

"White."

"License number?" He kept prodding.

"Smoke, I–"

"I know you know it." I heard Smoke push numbers on a land phone, then relay my information to communications.

I tried to visualize the license plate, but the numbers and letters weren't readable.

"Come on Corky, you can do it. You memorize license numbers as a matter of course. It's your irritating, endearing habit," Smoke added with a lighter tone.

The plate would not focus. "I'm trying. Don't talk for a minute and I'll concentrate." I closed my eyes and saw the white Cadillac with the hood up. I glanced at the plate. G-4-8-2-A-2.

"George, Four, Eight, Two, Adam, Two."

A loud exhale sounded in my ear. "That's my girl. I knew you could do it. Stay with me. I'm leaving my house and I'll be talking to communications on my work cell. I'll be in my squad car in a sec. You know I won't leave you."

"I know."

"Corky? An APB is going out as we speak, and communications says the registered owner is a Gregory Parker of Hamel. Parker's DOB makes him fifty-three. Five-foot-nine, one-ninety, gray hair, hazel eyes."

Parker. Hamel.

"No, that doesn't fit the guy on my road. I'm trying to put something together."

First one image, then another, took shape in my mind's eye. A bearded man with longish brown hair, glancing up at me with look that made me uneasy. A clean shaven man with the same cold, green-eyed stare, a split second before he knocked me over the head. I swallowed, trying to expunge an acidy, bitter taste from my mouth.

"Parker, different first name. I stopped him near Wolf Lake a few days after we found Molly. Scary eyes. Green. Name? Langdon, no Langley."

"Corky, I just walked into communications. We got Minneapolis P.D., Hamel P.D., and Hennepin County all on the horn. I got one officer running Langley Parker and Jerry just handed me the list of the other vehicles registered to Gregory Parker. They include a 2008 Ford Expedition and an A-1 horse trailer."

"Oh, God!"

"Langley owns a silver Lexus and a tan Chevy Malibu."

"Smoke!" Panic surrounded me in the dark space.

"Just stay focused, little lady. Hamel is sending a cop, and Hennepin will have at least two squads at the Parker residence as back-up, in case we somehow miss him along the way. There are three possible routes he could take and we're diverting every deputy we can to those roads."

"I'm leaving as we speak to travel the most likely one: Highway 55. He couldn't drive as fast as I do if he tried. What's the surface of the road you're on?"

Smooth. I recognized the sound under the tires. "Blacktop."

"Good. Any stops?"

I had to think back to my first moment of consciousness. "No."

"Good. My guess is you're between Oak Lea and Rockville. Most direct route. I'll call our 120 unit to take a stationary position along the highway."

A blackness threatened to envelope me. "I'm so scared and so sleepy."

"Stay with me, Corinne. You have all the skills

necessary for any situation. Remember that," he reminded me.

"Smoke! He's turning, taking a right on a gravel road!"

"Find a weapon. You got a weapon?"

I reached around the trunk. I felt a roll of rope, an empty canvas bag, a tire iron.

Bingo.

I gripped it close to me. "Yes. I got the tire iron."

Beep!

"Good."

Beep!

"Smoke, my battery's low, my phone's dying. I'm going to shut it off so I have a little left to call you back."

"Corky, don't–"

I tucked my phone into my pocket, and prayed for clarity of mind and strength of body, to handle whatever was in store for me. My adrenal glands released a massive dose of epinephrine when the car rolled to a stop and I heard the driver's door slam shut. I'm not ashamed to admit I would have wet my pants if I had had anything to drink that morning.

I tried to ignore my thumping heart and the pulses hammering from every pore of my body. My panting was drying out my cottony mouth and I resisted the urge to cough. I willed every system in my body to concentrate on facing the demon who was coming for me.

Thank God I had enough space to crouch on my feet and hands. When the trunk popped open, I sprang from my stooped position, a little too fast, and knocked the top of my head on the hood. I blinked in shock as I felt a tug on the tire iron. It started to slip out of my right hand, so I reached up, and with all of my strength, stuck the ring and pointer fingers of my left hand into Parker's hate-filled eyes. Eyes the color of a dark forest.

Parker's head recoiled and his grasp on the iron loosened a tad. I reached over with my left hand, and using the force of my body, punched the tire iron into his throat. He stumbled backward and a low, choking "aghagh" sound finally came out of his open mouth.

His bulging eyes stared at me as I jumped to the ground. I was released from my prison at last.

"Get down! Lie flat on your belly! Now!" I ordered.

He clenched his fists, and the muscles in his neck grew taut and protruded from his skin. He wasn't giving up. He lunged for me, but I jumped to the right and danced from one foot to the next, like boxers do in the ring. The tire iron was heavy and it was getting more and more difficult to hold it up.

Parker was still struggling for breath when he came at me again. I took a leap to the right. His words weren't audible, but I knew he was cursing me.

Before he had a chance to turn, I pivoted around, holding the tire iron like a bat. I swung with every ounce of my one hundred and ten pounds. The heavy metal smacked the back of his knees and he dropped like an anchor. I wound up for another strike and drove a blow to his back, even harder than the first. I heard what had to have been ribs breaking, a muffled, cracking noise. He toppled forward, panting furiously to suck in what oxygen he could.

I kneeled into his left shoulder on the pressure point next to the blade. He reacted with a grunt, but couldn't move away. I didn't dare let go of the tire iron in case he somehow broke free. I managed to retrieve the phone from my pocket, turned it on, and hit the "1".

"Dammit, Corky—"

I recognized a farm in the distance

"We're a mile west of Rockville, south on Edward."

"I'm less than two miles away."

How long could I hold on? "Hurry, Smoke."

I had never been happier to hear sirens in my entire life. Zubinksi was the Rockville car and drove in on Smoke's bumper, followed by a Minnesota State Patrol officer who was in the area.

All three had their guns drawn as they approached. Smoke signaled Mandy and the trooper to train their guns on Parker.

"Mr. Parker, if you make one move, you will be shot in the head. Do you understand?" Smoke yelled.

Parker surprised me by answering. "Yes," he choked out.

Smoke moved in from behind us, grabbed Parker's right hand, pulled it back, and applied handcuffs. He knelt on the sciatic nerve in Parker's butt. Parker flinched and shrieked.

I looked over my shoulder at Smoke, and when he motioned to the left, I rolled away. He cuffed Parker's other hand.

"Either one of you got leg irons?" Smoke asked Zubinski and Trooper Weller.

"I do," Weller said. He had them on Parker in under a minute.

Smoke and Weller got Parker to his feet, but he couldn't straighten up.

"I think I broke his rib."

All three of them looked at me and each smiled in a covert way.

Smoke pulled the radio from his belt. "340, Winnebago County."

"Go ahead 340."

"We're code four with one male in custody. Send a tow to our location."

"10-4." There was obvious relief in Jerry's voice.

Parker lifted his head and glared at me, sending waves of emotions throughout my body.

"It isn't over," Parker snarled.

Smoke lunged toward him. Zubinski and Weller both reacted, ready to prevent an altercation, but Smoke stopped himself before he made contact with Parker's body.

Smoke's jaw was clenched and his lips barely moved. "Let's get this low-life into your squad, Zubinski. We better get him checked out at the hospital so the jail won't be liable in case his lung is punctured."

Parker wouldn't look at any of us after that. He kept his eyes fixed on the ground. The injury and leg irons made it difficult to negotiate him into the small back seat of the squad car, but they managed. Trooper Weller buckled him in.

Another Winnebago County squad car pulled up, adding to the growing line of vehicles on the gravel road.

Todd Mason frowned when he saw me. I realized I must have looked a mess.

"I can follow Deputy Zubinski to the hospital," Trooper Weller offered.

"Good. I'll get two more deputies to meet you there. Mason, will you wait for the tow? I'm taking Corky in to get checked out."

I wasn't going to argue. I felt weak, dizzy, and started to shiver.

"Sure." Mason glanced into Zubinski's squad car and shook his head. "Didn't figure him for a skinhead."

I was about to tell Mason the shaved head was a recent change for Parker, but my teeth started to chatter. Smoke tuned in to my physical condition and put his arm around my shoulder.

"Mason, Zubinski, got a blanket in your car?"

"Sure, it's even clean." Mason handed a wool blanket to Smoke and he wrapped it around me.

"Mason, take some photos of the scene: the vehicle, tire iron, trunk, scuffle marks on the gravel—they won't show up well, but get 'em anyway. You can put the iron back in the trunk and we'll process it with the rest of the vehicle. You'll follow the tow, get the vehicle secured in the garage?"

Mason nodded. "Yes sir."

"Okay, let's get a move on."

Zubinksi and Weller backed their squads down the slight embankment to turn around.

"What an ordeal. Corky, are you okay?" Mason asked.

I shook my head 'no.' "But, I will be."

"Am I hurting you?" Smoke asked as he guided me to his car.

I shook my head again. "Pretty numb still."

Smoke tensed slightly then eased his hold as he assisted me into the passenger seat. He reached across me for the seatbelt, drew it gently across my body, and snapped it in the lock. My right arm wouldn't move, but I caught the back of his bicep with my left hand and pulled him in until my face rested in the crook of his neck. I felt his pulse and breath quicken. He didn't move for a moment, then pulled back to look into my eyes.

"I almost killed that bastard." Smoke's voice was quiet and intense.

One tear, then another, ran down my cheek, but I had no words.

"We'll talk about all this later. Right now we have to get you to the hospital. It looks like a pretty good-sized goose egg on the side of your head." Smoke's low, calm tone didn't fool me. His muscles were tight and I knew a host of emotions were raging inside him.

I leaned my head back and closed my eyes.

"Corky, stay awake," Smoke instructed as he slid behind the wheel.

"I'm just so tired. I want to go to sleep."

"You gotta stay awake. I'm sure you've got a concussion, maybe a fracture."

"In this thick skull of mine?" My lips curled up slightly.

"Well, you can be very hard-headed, at times. Least you didn't get your sense of humor knocked out of you." Smoke's detective squad car was not equipped with a light bar, but he had a flashing light for emergencies. It was clamped on the top of his car.

Smoke activated his siren and I let out an "Ow!"

"Sorry. I don't want to hurt your head any more, but I'm not driving the speed limit. Can you pull the blanket over your ears, muffle the noise?"

"I'll be okay. It'll help keep me awake."

40.

I drifted in and out of consciousness for two days in a lavender-colored hospital room. I had fleeting thoughts of how much my Grandma Brandt had loved both the shade and the scent of lavender, and how much I missed her. Every time I woke up there seemed to be another bouquet of flowers and someone new sitting beside me.

I had maintained a stage three concussion and hairline fracture from the tire iron blow and, although it wasn't serious, the doctors wanted to keep me resting quietly for a few days. Whatever drug they mingled with the intravenous fluids made me sleep a lot.

Once, when I blinked awake for minute, Nick was holding my hand in both of his. Another time, my mother and grandparents were sitting as a group, their worried faces staring at me. Smoke, Sara, Sheriff Twardy, Mandy Zubinski, Carlson, Mason, Weber, and too many deputies to count, were there on different occasions.

I woke up on Monday aware of the fading late afternoon sun on my face and a hand resting on my arm.

"Hello, little lady," the familiar, melodious voice crooned.

My eyes blinked closed. "Detective Dawes."

"How are you doing? Tired of sleeping, yet?"

"Isn't that like an oxymoron, tired of sleeping?" A smile tugged at my face.

He snickered. "Could be. I finally convinced your mother to go home for a while, told her I'd sit with you. She said they're weaning you off the sedatives, so you'll be awake more."

"Good, although I haven't minded the break from thinking and processing everything that happened." A brief retreat from reality.

I felt his breath near my ear. "Are you feeling any

better?"

"My head hurts. Of course. But, I gotta say, since I actually lived through the very worst day of my life, I am mostly feeling just plain grateful." That was it.

His hand was heavy on my shoulder. "Corky, truth be told, I have to say it was the worst day of my life, too." He made a 'humph' sound. "I expect my hair to turn completely gray by Friday."

A man accustomed to stress.

"You didn't think you'd get me in time, did you?"

"Oh, no, I knew we would." I saw him cross his fingers to cover his lie. "But you should consider less dramatic ways to capture criminals."

"Really? You think being threatened in my own home with a gun, or getting knocked over the head, thrown in a trunk, and driven away, is dramatic?"

"A little over the top, yes."

"I will strive for less drama." The image of my captor's wild, hate-filled eyes came to mind. "Tell me about Parker."

"He is our monster, all right, but you should heal some more before you get all the gory particulars."

"I've got a lot of the 'gory particulars' on this case already." I pushed on his chest. "I need to know."

Smoke didn't answer right away. "Parker's locked up in the Hennepin County Jail, in segregation, mainly for medical reasons, but also for keeping an eye on his mental status. You were right when you thought you cracked his rib—you cracked two of 'em. You should've cracked his skull, like he cracked yours. Justifiable use of deadly force, in my book. Sergeant, you were badly injured, in danger of passing out again. Definitely justifiable to use deadly force."

Easy to say, after the fact. "I guess. If he hadn't gone down with that back strike, I would have gone for a spine or head strike. I was relying solely on my training. My brain was pretty rattled at the time."

"Corky, when we moved in to make the arrest, I was so overwhelmed with the need to shoot that depraved you-know-what, I had to holster my gun because I was convinced I would kill him if I didn't."

I squeezed his hand.

Smoke searched my face before going on. "We got four jurisdictions bringing charges against him: Minneapolis P.D., Hennepin County—since rural Hamel is theirs—and Winnebago. And the feds want him on the kidnapping charges. That's where he'll get fried."

"What'd they find at his house? Evidence-wise?"

"Turns out Special Agent Erley was right on. His parents have a hobby farm in Hamel, and he has a loft in the warehouse district of Minneapolis. It was no problem getting expedited search warrants after he made the stupid mistake of kidnapping a Winnebago County sergeant."

I sensed Smoke was stalling. "And?"

"I went to the farm with Hennepin and Minneapolis. No one was home, but we batted a thousand, anyway. Tire tracks on the Expedition and horse trailer matched those found at Lake Pearl State Park. And there were ten horses, Arabians, at the farm. One had hooves that fit those found at the shoreline of Wolf Lake. BCA confirmed all this today. They took the Expedition to the BCA, since we got so many jurisdictions involved. They're combing through it."

My mind filled with images of the Engens, the leg lying on their lawn, Wolf Lake, hoof prints, divers, body parts.

Smoke's face was close. "You okay?"

"Yeah, go on," I invited.

"While we were there, a guy who tends to the horses showed up and said Parker's parents would be home the next afternoon. Hennepin waited for 'em and then took 'em in for questioning. They apparently knew nothing. They're gone a lot. Sounds like they've always been gone a lot. They left their son with his grandparents on a regular basis when he was young. Guess where?"

The pieces were falling together. "The farmhouse where the Engens live on Wolf Lake?"

"You got it."

"So what happened at that farm that made him leave a dismembered body there?" I wondered.

Smoke shook his head. "We'll keep digging. Grandparents are still alive, but in assisted living. Sounds like Parker was always a little different, according to the parents—kept to himself, no real friends. But they never saw this coming. He's got a good position. He's a laboratory geneticist at the Veterinary Diagnostic Laboratory at the University of Minnesota."

"You have got to be kidding me!"

"He's not dumb. Remember, psychotics wear lots of different hats and look like you and me."

I tried to process it all. "Did he kill Molly at his parents' farm?"

"No, it was at his loft."

A nurse came into the room, checked my vital signs, and the fluids in the IV bottle. "Very good. Pulse, fifty-five, BP is one-ten over sixty. Is there anything I can get for you?"

"No thanks." I returned her smile.

The nurse checked my water pitcher, then left.

Smoke studied my face. "Corky, you're tired. We can finish this later. The sheriff will have my hide if he finds out I've told you all this when you're supposed to be resting. I think your mother's protective influence is rubbing off on him."

"Oh great." At least my mother had someone to help ease her stress. "Smoke, just tell me—I'm not going to rat you out to the sheriff."

Smoke looked at his palms for a minute. "Going through Parker's loft was an experience I don't want to repeat in this lifetime."

"Why, what'd you find?"

"He had video equipment set up. Tapes, a bed where he kept his victims bound, evidence of torture and rape, the saw he used to dismember them, a couple of duffle bags to transport their body parts."

I felt my stomach tighten, then churn. "Them?

How many?"

"Evidence of two. There's positive proof the other missing prostitute, Amber Ferman, was another of Parker's victims."

Amber Ferman. I waited for Smoke to go on, but he remained silent. "What positive proof?"

Smoke lifted an eyebrow. "In addition to the tapes, we found both of the victims' heads in Parker's freezer."

I was silent as I imagined opening the freezer door. "That's why we couldn't find Molly's head. Oh!" I was thankful I had missed the loft search. "Okay, so, now they have Ferman's head, but where's her body?"

Smoke shrugged. "Don't know yet. Parker's not sayin' much."

"Did you interview him?"

"After they taped him up here at the hospital, we booked him in our jail. Detective Harrison and I had at him for close to three hours, but he didn't break. Had his first appearance this morning in front of Judge Davidson, got charged with kidnapping, assault with a deadly weapon, interference with a dead body, trespass."

Smoke made a 'huh' sound at the last charge. Trespass did not adequately describe what Parker did when he rode his horse to the edge of Wolf Lake and threw Molly's remains into the water.

"After his appearance, we took him to Hennepin and I sat in when both Minneapolis and Hennepin investigators interrogated him. That went on another couple of hours. Then he appeared in district court there, and got charged with a long list: kidnapping, assault, rape, murder, yada, yada. The FBI will have at it tomorrow. It's a complex process, that's for sure."

I yawned before I could stifle it. "I just can't understand how he could do what he did." I felt myself quiver. "Was he going to do the same thing to me?"

Smoke reached over and squeezed my hands. "I don't know. Truth is, my mind won't let me go there." He watched me for a while. "You really do need to rest."

I still had questions. "Is my mom okay? Grandma, Grandpa, Gramps?"

"It's hard to hide the facts from your mother and grandmother. You're grandma is a natural investigator and your mom is like a mother bear protecting her young."

"Oh, really?"

We both smiled.

"And John Carl is flying up this weekend to see you."

I nodded, remembering my mother telling me that when I was half awake. "That'll be good for Mom, too."

Smoke reached over and put his hand over my eyes. "Now, go to sleep."

41.

A week of daytime temperatures in low seventies gave us a warm reprieve from the average mid-October highs in the fifties. Walkers and joggers were out in shorts and tee shirts. It made me long to be medically cleared to resume all my normal activities. Sara stopped at my house Friday when she finished work.

"Sure you don't want to come to Brainerd with me this weekend? My folks are hoping you'll change your mind."

"It would be fun, but I don't want to cancel my date with Nick tonight. He's cooking." I raised my eyebrows.

"Lucky girl. How are your headaches?"

"Actually, about gone. I haven't taken any ibuprofen for the last two days."

"Good. So you heard Eisner got sentenced, huh?"

"Yeah, Smoke called to tell me she'd been transported to Shakopee Women's Prison to live out her few remaining days."

Sara gave me a hug. "It's been a hard few months, hasn't it? And how is Rebecca doing?"

Rebecca, the little girl in my heart. "I think really well. I called her after school today and she was sad about her grandmother, but overall, sounded pretty happy."

"When are you planning to tell her about her great-grandmother?"

I gave her an incredulous look and shrugged. "Ah, never? I don't know. The Brenners and I thought we should let the dust settle, get through the adoption process."

"I think that's a good idea. How are you doing with the nightmares? Still having bad ones?" Sara leaned in for a closer look at me.

"Here and there. The psychologist is really helping me work through it all."

"Are you scared to go back on the road? I know I would be." She pulled a glass from the cupboard and filled it with water.

"A little. That's why I'm so anxious to get released by the doc. I see him on Monday. The sheriff says he'll keep me on light duty as long as necessary, but I'm already tired of pushing papers, after only one week." I drummed my hands on my thigh. "I just want to be in my squad car again."

Sara put her hands on mine to still them. "You got injured only three weeks ago tomorrow, it's not like you've been laid up forever."

I shrugged. "It seems like forever. But I understand, from a medical point of view. I mean, I don't want any setbacks, so I am minding my P's and Q's. For now."

"All in due time, huh?"

"That's what they say."

42.

Langley had about all he could stand from investigators. If his mother came to visit one more time, he would be sick. He had to become famous to get her to actually notice him.

Jail was no problem. Everyone knew who he was and gave him as much space as he needed. He kept to himself, like he always had. The worst part was the corrections officer-Eve who served as housing officer every so often. That's when he missed his freedom. Fantasies didn't satisfy his urges.

Langley was surprised by the number of letters he had gotten in the past weeks, mostly from young women— and a few men—offering friendship and more. A note from a work colleague both relieved and troubled him. A researcher in another state had stumbled upon the cause and cure of CA. Langley had always believed he would be the one to win that distinction. But, for Sheik's sake, he was glad it was found.

Sheik. What would he do without his faithful master, his Gideon? He might die of loneliness. All because Langley got interrupted before he could bind and gag the Eve-cop. He could barely comprehend what had happened. He didn't let himself think about it much because hot waves of failure and humiliation would roll over him until sweat erupted from his pores and dampened his skin.

Langley hadn't finished his quest and wouldn't give up until he did. He'd find a way to put an end to the Eve-cop. He'd get one of his new groupies to help him.

43.

Nick drew me into his arms for a long and longing kiss. We stood with our arms wrapped around each other, swaying gently, like willows in the wind. "You hungry?"

"You say that like you're not talking about food." I smiled and his eyebrows raised in mock surprise.

"Faith is gone for the night," he hinted. "In the meantime, let me rephrase my previous question. Would you like to eat? You feel thinner."

"I lost a few pounds, but they're coming back. And, yes, I'd love to dine with you." I looked around the room.

"It's been so warm, I thought about eating outside, but as soon as the sun goes down, it cools off so fast."

"Yes, it does." Nick had his dining room table set with fine china, silver, and crystal on a linen table cloth. "I am so underdressed."

He stepped in behind me and clasped his arms around my middle. "I love you in jeans, although I have to admit, that little black dress you wore last month about knocked my socks off."

I laughed, then felt immediate guilt, remembering the response it had drawn from Smoke. I was glad Nick couldn't see my face. He reached around me and pulled a chair away from the table.

"Madam." Nick guided me to my place at the table. He lifted a bottle of pinot grigio from the table cooler and poured a splash in my glass as a sample.

"Very nice."

"It pleases you?"

"Yes, thank you," I said as he added wine to my glass.

"I will be right back." Nick returned seconds later with a salad of baby greens, almonds, and mushrooms,

drizzled with a vinaigrette.

"Sure beats hospital food," I teased between bites of steak tenderloin and twice-baked potatoes.

Nick's expression grew dark, like a storm cloud had moved in.

"What is it?" I asked.

His voice was grim. "Finish eating, then we'll talk."

I could barely choke down the last of my food. Nick rose, took my hand, and led me into the living room. We sat side by side on the couch.

"I can't tell you how difficult it was seeing you lying in that hospital bed day after day. What is happening with the case?" Nick's brown eyes were intense, nearly black. I was momentarily stunned by his words and his look.

"Um, not much right now. He's been charged with crimes in three venues, by four different jurisdictions. He may not get to trial in Hennepin, or Federal Court, for up to a year, maybe longer. Winnebago? Probably less than a year."

Nick looked at my hands before raising his eyes to mine. "I didn't think you'd go back after what happened."

"To work, you mean?" He nodded and I shrugged. "It's my job. More than my job, it's my career."

He shook his head slowly. "Corky, I can't do this anymore."

"Do what?" I asked, my heart picking up its pace, waiting.

"Going through hell every day you're at work—wondering if you're okay, frightened beyond all reason something will happen to you. And things do happen, so I guess it's not an unreasonable fear."

The conversation didn't seem real. "Nick, I don't know what to say."

He reached over and grasped my arm. "How about you'll leave the sheriff's department and marry me?"

That came out of left field. "Nick—"

"You need some time to think about it?" His handsome face was earnest.

I shook my head. "I never thought our relationship

would come to a choice between marriage and my profession. Is that fair? Would you leave your job to marry me?" I pulled back from him.

"That's different."

"How?"

"I am not in threat of my life on a regular basis."

"Neither am I, Nick. Granted, there did happen to be two threats this year, but normally, things are pretty routine around here."

He picked up my hands and softened his voice. "Corky. I'm not an ultimatum kind of guy, but I can't change my feelings. I lost one wife, I don't know if I'd survive losing another." I squeezed his hands to offer some sympathy. "And it's not just me—there's Faith. It would devastate her to have another mother die."

"Nick, anyone can die at anytime. You know there are no guarantees. Death is a fact of life."

He pulled me gently in his arms. "I know how much your career means to you. I just hoped I meant more."

"That's not fair, Nick."

He eased me to an arm's length and held my eyes with his for a long time. "Maybe not, but that's the way it is."

"Is this goodbye?" My voice was strained and I swallowed hard.

Nick's eyes grew misty and he nodded as a tear rolled down his cheek.

44.

Smoke was sitting on his dock. The moon was full overhead and a kerosene lantern rested on one of the dock's poles.

"Why are you out here in the cold?" I asked as I approached him.

"Cold? It's close to fifty degrees."

"After the warm Indian summer day we had, it feels nippy," I said.

I sat on the bench next to Smoke and watched him cast then reel in his line.

He gave me a sideways glance. "I thought you had a date tonight?"

"I did until I got dumped."

He turned toward me. "Dumped? As in, Nick broke up with you?"

I couldn't speak so I nodded.

"What happened?" He set his fishing pole down.

I swallowed, hoping the lump in my throat would go down. "He . . . couldn't . . . take . . . it . . . me . . . being . . . a . . ."

"Cop?"

"He . . . made . . . me . . . choose." Tears spilled out of my eyes.

"Come here." Smoke locked his arm around my shoulder and pulled me close. "You're shivering." He bought his other arm around the front of me and rubbed to warm me up. "Let's go inside."

"It's . . . fine."

"You sure?"

I nodded.

We sat in silence for a time before Smoke spoke again. "You know, not that Nick's right, but I can understand how he might feel. You've had some pretty close calls over the last few months. Probably didn't know what he was signing up for, dating a cop."

I shrugged.

"You want to talk about it?"

My tears had stopped and I shook my head. "Not tonight."

"You going to get through this?"

I nodded.

"Got any plans of what to do next?"

"There is something I've been thinking about for a while."

"What's that?"

"I'm going to get a dog. A big watchdog that likes to go on long runs."

He squeezed a little tighter. "Mighty fine plan."

"Will you help me find a good one? One like Rex?"

I felt Smoke nod. "I think I can handle that. We'll get on it, a-sap."

Also by Christine Husom:

Murder in Winnebago County

Slowly, meticulously, Sgt. Corky Aleckson
is piecing it all together—the deaths of the
judge, the public defender and the
prosecutor are all connected. What she
hasn't figured out is who else the serial
killer is after and why . . . or that her
investigation has put her on the murderer's
list as well.

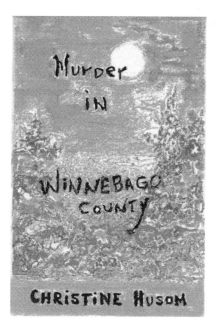

Available from

WWW.SECONDWINDPUBLISHING.COM
Other Mystery / Crime titles available from